I AM ONLY MARY

2nd Edition

THOMAS W. ATZBERGER

Cover by:
Sherri Rinderle

TABLE OF CONTENTS

†

BEGINNINGS

"The edge of the earth glows again, Acha," said his hunting partner, Onyo.

Acha responded, "Again, there are no clouds. Even at this early part of the day, breathing is warm in our throats."

"Yes, and the water already runs from me. It runs down my back, and off my face, and falls onto the dust." said Onyo.

"We are wet, and the earth is dry," Acha said. "It is good to be a hunting man and to go again from our caves to the grasslands."

As they walked out from the dwelling area, Acha said, "I look at the animals. They are brothers to me. The animals are beautiful. I have always wanted to be one of them, to walk anywhere I want and live everywhere."

Onyo said, "I remember when the older men took us out the hunt for the first time. They hunted so well. They showed me how to chip the stones and to throw them. Many days we lived away from the caves and followed the animals. When I took my first animal, they praised me and, in the evening, they proclaimed me a man and gave me the name 'Onyo,' because that was the sound I made when I threw my stone."

"Yes, Onyo. It was the same for me and for our fathers, and their fathers. It will be the same for our sons and their sons. It will be that way for ever." Onyo said, "The day is good. The animals will not hide today."

"True," said Acha. "It is early; The sun is not yet angry."

They walked on. Acha was a thinker, and usually did not speak unless he was spoken to first. Onyo was an imaginer; he would speak often, but with shallow insight.

Onyo said, "I often want to walk and walk far beyond here. I think of what is at the end of the land, or the great salty water where the sun goes down each night. What do you think is there farther than we can see?"

Acha answered, "I do not know," because he did not know.

Onyo said "I worry that someday the sun will not rise. I wonder if the sun is a creature like an animal that runs through the sky, like a large bird."

Acha answered, "I have never seen it move from its track, and so it does not seem to be a being like an animal. If it is a being, it is a creature much nobler than we are; it is far more trustworthy than many of us. I am happy when I see it come back each day."

Onyo said, "We have moved a sun-width's walk from the caves. Often here we begin to see the animals, eating the grasses. Do you have your three stones?"

"Yes," said Acha. "I made two new ones yesterday. Look. I hit my finger with the hitting stone as I was chipping the throwing stone."

Onyo looked with sympathetic smile at his friend's small wound. They walked on some time without speaking. Acha finally said, "The stones are powerful. They bring death to the animal very quickly when we throw them well."

Onyo said, "Where do you think this land came from? How long has it been here?"

Acha responded, "I believe that it was put here for us by a great being. No one else could do so much."

Onyo said, "Truly He is a very great being. A Great Hidden being. I would like to meet Him."

Acha said, "He does not show himself to us. We only see what He has made. For me, that is beautiful enough."

Onyo said, "I wonder if he ever helps us."

Acha made no response.

Eventually Acha said, "The animals have been by here. See, the grasses are chewed and their droppings are fresh."

"The breeze grows stronger," said Onyo. "Still, it is hot to breathe."

Soon, Onyo whispered intensely, "I see them far across the plain."

Acha responded, "Yes, I see them too. We will eat well this day. It is a very good day."

Onyo said, "The breeze takes away our smell and covers our noises. Yes, we will do well today."

Acha then said, "We must move away from each other now. If the herd runs, we will have a better chance to take an animal if we are not together. I will watch you and sign to you that I see you. We should try to attack at the same time."

Onyo crept ever closer, making as little noise as possible. He could still see Acha on the far side of the herd. The breeze burbled in their ears, and they knew it would help mask the rustling of the grasses. Finally, Onyo knelt, and watched and waited. He contemplated the animals, as he did each time he hunted. He breathed their familiar, sour scent. He watched them eat. He felt them think when they looked up, chewing, evaluating their own safety. When satisfied with the situation, the animals walked a bit this way or that, to another patch of grass to eat. He sympathized with them about the flies that bothered them and caused their tails and ears and flanks to be in motion all the time. As he waited, he felt the luxury of knowing he had nothing else to do but wait. It was this way for his forebears and it would be this way for his progeny, for centuries in either direction. This was his life, the relationship that he and these animals were made for.

As they grazed their way in his direction, he planned which one to take. It was important to take the biggest one possible. It was also important to take an antlered male; it carried with it the status of winning out over danger. The other men would respect that.

Eventually, as he edged through the grasses, ever closer to the herd, the time to act arrived. He looked over toward Acha and raised his hand; Acha raised his in return. The hunt was on.

As he had so many times before, he slowly pulled his knees under him, sitting on his feet and leaning low on his hands. He took a stone from the pouch and gripped it well. He pulled his left foot forward, still keeping low, and brought his knee just beside his face. He gripped his stone, focused on the ear of his chosen target, a young but worthy male. He would rise as quickly and, at the same time, as quietly as he could, to get his throw in before the herd started and dashed off. In one graceful move he transformed thought into action, concentrating on his point of impact, rising to his feet and throwing his stone with all of his might, factoring in how it might drift and turn on its way.

On this day, his calculations were as good as ever, but his luck was not. The animal, at the same time, chose to step forward for a new bite of the grass. The stone hit him in the shoulder, bruising him deeply and chipping a bone but not, by any means, bringing him down.

The animal leapt high in its surprise, and the rest of the herd bolted as one with the pelting sound of a hailstorm. The man seized another stone and pursued his quarry as fast as he could. The animal tried to run, but its shoulder hurt more than it had ever experienced. It turned, instead, to fight. Now they were in a relationship to each other. The animal sized up the man and lowered his sharp antlers, his only tools, to menace the man. The man tried to move slowly to a side vantage point on the animal, but, of course, the animal turned with him. The man's strategy now was to get as close as possible, and throw his second stone to the animal's forehead. Closeness was crucial, even if the animal charged. A charge would simply shorten the time to wait to throw the stone. At the same time, the man must be ready to dodge the sharp antlers.

The man watched closely, his mind effectively blending with the animal's through the subtle signals the animal gave. Onyo recognized that the animal's adrenalin coursed through in its veins, and could see that the pain in its shoulder and the ire in its mind burned together. Onyo knew that the animal saw him as the source of its pain, and as its enemy. He saw the tensing of the animal's muscles and the breaths it took; he could feel its moment of decision. As the animal charged, the man drew back and threw his sharpened stone. It flew very briefly, almost instantly, between the man and the animal, and hit the animal in the center of the forehead. It was a solid blow that imparted all of its force. It did not glance off but, drained of its inertia, dropped from the head of the running animal and rolled lazily on the ground. Rage still controlled the animal, and the stone did not interrupt his charge. He still drove towards the man with his knives of horn. The man continued to turn with the inertia of his throw, hoping to roll to the left of the animal as it passed. However, he was just a bit slow to be out of the way and the animal's right rack caught the man's left upper back as he rolled. The animal did not get a solid blow. Still, it had cut the man in a number of places on his shoulder.

Onyo knew it gratified the animal to make this contact with his foe and he saw the animal turn to find him again and press the attack. During the attack, the crack in the animal's skull and the bleeding within it had not yet registered with him. But now, things were odd. Onyo wondered if the outer edges of the animal's vision were sparkly and indefinite, as had happened to him once when he stuck his head in a fall. Onyo could see that the animal faced a difficulty it did not recognize; it tried to shake it off. He saw that the animal did not have any more a clear idea of what to do. He tried to move his feet but they were mostly unresponsive.

The man could see that the animal's life was slowly draining away. The animal stared at the man. Soon, the animal's eyes were not looking at anything and it slowly fell into the grass, its life gone, and its usefulness to the man fully realized.

The man was angry with himself about his wounds; he should have been quicker. Now the task of moving the animal would be much more difficult, to say nothing of the laughter the other men would enjoy at his expense. He looked around and gathered up the two stones he had used. Working through the pain, he rolled the animal on its back and crouched under the antlers. He stood with his own shoulders under the antlers and began to drag the animal back to the living area, many steps towards the sun's rising place. It would take about as long as it does for the sun to move from first showing to being fully up, a morning sun-width.

While his hunting had been successful, the man was far from victory. He could not yet enjoy his prize. He looked for Acha, but did not see him. Often, the chasing of the bolting herd would take the hunting partner far afield and that was what he recognized about today. Acha would find his way back, probably with a prize of his own.

Onyo had to keep a wary eye on his surroundings while he carried the heavy animal home. This was a very vulnerable time. He knew that the stones worked on men as well as on the animals. Nor was he the only one who knew of the power these stones carried. He had no concern for whether he could make it home; the pain was just a bother.

As wary as he was, and as experienced as he was, he did not yet see another man who had watched him all morning from a safe distance, hiding in the grasses, as the hunters had done originally, to stalk their prey. With the herd now dispersed somewhat, the stranger was faced with a choice to either follow the herd or to take Onyo's prize from him. If other men were not in sight, the stranger might be able to carry it off. There was the risk that the victim might be an able warrior. There was the risk of being caught by Onyo's clan or of their suspecting the robber's identity and clan. There was the risk of revenge.

Over the centuries, many others in similar circumstances had tried one avenue or the other. Some would follow the herd, and secure their own prize, or not. Others would choose ambush and theft, and would be successful, or not. This was another of the countless days on the face of the earth where men and other living things made their decisions and lived, or died, by them.

✝

THE VILLAGE

Perhaps a million days after pre-historic hunters stalked grazing beasts in the grasses of this land, the hot blanket of yet another unrestrained sunrise lay over it. It again warmed the shoulders and backs of people. Over this large time, generations upon generations of people had made many changes: they domesticated animals, mastered farming, developed laws and organized their communities.

This day, Hannah and Esther, and their little daughters, were on their way to the village market. The chalky dust of the village lane puffed from under their feet as they walked. Hannah's child, Mary, and Esther's child, Ruth, toddled along with them.

"You look pretty in your cotton tunic, Mary," said Hannah. "This color is white and this little stripe at the bottom is blue. Your headscarf is also white," she said, perfecting its arrangement on the little girl's head.

Hannah's view of her little three-year-old caught on small, endearing jewels of sweat on her golden cheeks, just under her olive brown eyes. The woman looked a while at this child, so small yet so much a person already, able to walk on tiny feet and legs, able to talk with her tiny voice, able to think her own thoughts with her baby mind. In the mother's heart, this child and her needs were the reason for living.

"These children are so dear, aren't they Esther?" said Hannah. The women had no sense of the forces of culture, natural resources, or science. For each of them, it was an unquestioning living of a role she had learned by observation and tradition. The work of caring for her child gave her great satisfaction. At the same time, it blended with the great burden of leading the child in growing up. Each mother in her own way added this moment to the others that she knew would remain in her mind over the years.

Mary suddenly stopped and turned to her mother with her arms up. Ruth immediately saw the wisdom of such an idea, and did the same. The mothers each reached down and picked up her child. Each girl took her familiar place on her mother's hip, and each mother, in turn, craned her head back some to look at her little girl and they shared a small quiet smile. The mothers were quite willing to carry the children now; there would be walking enough for the little girls on the way back from the market.

"I am so happy to be a mother," said Hannah. "It took so long for the Lord to answer my prayers. I remember how my mother taught me the tasks of womanhood, of caring for the house, of tending to the children, and of caring for the wounds one's husband may suffer in the daily commerce of the village. I love teaching Mary these things"

"Yes," said Esther. "It is a special place we have in our families. I have seen many girls in this village become women, become betrothed and married, give birth, and take their places in the neighborhood. It is beautiful to watch life flow from one generation to the next."

Esther went on, "I remember when I first realized that womanhood would be different from childhood, you now, in my body, I mean. My mother was really helpful about it. She taught me how to deal with the religious and practical concerns that came with it."

Hannah said, "In my years, I have seen many different situations. Some women have had very hard lives, with insensitive husbands who constantly criticized their homes and their labors, or did worse things to them. Some others have lost their husbands and have had nothing to depend on but the charity of their families and neighbors. So many have died in childbirth and are now only memories in my heart. Some have children with special shortcomings and problems, making their mothers' work more challenging."

"Yes," said Esther. It is bitter and sweet to realize that all of the elements of life will unfold in the future of these children in some way. Each will have her own experiences in the history of her own family, friends, neighbors, and even strangers. I would love to be able to control every danger they face, but we cannot."

"True," said Hannah. "In fact it would not be good for them if we did that. Our own example will be the best way our daughters will learn what they will need to live their own lives and raise their own children."

As they came closer to the square of the village, the women left their discussion and turned to more practical things. They entered the square, more an area than an architectural feature. Again this day, the sounds and aromas and images presented by the vendors gave them a familiar sense of health and newness. They parted and went off, each in search of her own items to purchase.

At the center of this village life was the well. Young men might pass by intentionally to catch a glimpse of the young women who came to the well every day to gather their household's water.

It was here that people met and shared news, perhaps a little gossip, and advice, and planned to assist each other in times of weddings and childbirth, diseases and dying. Relationships were woven around the well. It would be here as much as at home that the child would learn how to live in the village.

Hannah went to the well and took her turn getting the day's water for her household. Mary asked her, "How does the water get into the well, Mommy?"

"It runs into it from deep in the ground," said Hannah.

Mary, being a child, asked next, "How does it get in the ground?"

"I think it gets there from the rain, and maybe from the snow of the mountains and the rivers. I'm just glad it is there," said Hannah.

"Can I see in the well?" said Mary.

Hannah looked at her child and contemplated her question. It was an interruption and a risky thing to do, but it would feed Mary's mind. Hannah decided that she could hold Mary carefully and let her learn this interesting thing.

"Alright, but I have to hold you very tight," said Hannah. "It is very deep, and there is water in the bottom. It would be very bad if you ever fell into this well. Are you sure you want to do this?"

Mary was only a little hesitant, as Hannah lifted her up and put both her arms tightly around Mary from behind. Mary and Hannah peered over the edge and down into the deep, dark tube of the well. There was the faintest glimmer of sky light off of the water. Mary was most impressed by the danger of this amazing thing, and Hannah could feel her start a bit at the realization.

"Isn't that interesting?" said Hannah.

Mary said nothing as Hannah put her back on solid ground, but the image of that foreboding tube stayed with her. Hannah said, "This well is very important to us, isn't it?" Mary was still contemplative and did not respond.

This was not a day when the mother and her daughter would journey the four miles between Nazareth and the larger, busier town of Zippori to see the wonderful things for sale there. After all, the offensive spirit of that Roman city was also palpable there, and diluted the pleasure of being in it. They would only go there if they needed something special. This was just another weekday, starting with a trip to the modest Nazareth market to gather the things they would need for the meals of the day: grains of wheat and barley, cucumbers, beans, lentils, onions, garlic, and olives for vegetables; grapes and figs for fruit; and some goat cheese and goat milk. Carrying the goods of the market, they began the walk back to their home. The sun was now higher and hotter, but they took little note. It was no different today than had been for many yesterdays. As they walked past neighbors' houses, some were coming out to go to the market or going home from their own walks there.

"Hello, Hannah," they would say.

"How are you today?"

"Oh, we are fine. We are just coming home from the market."

"And hello, Mary. How are you?"

Hannah had taught Mary how to respond to such polite questions.

"I am fine, thank you," she said in her baby voice.

The women would smile at each other, and the neighbor would say to Hannah, "What a dear child she is."

"Thank you," Hannah would say. "How is your family doing?"

Their discussions would cover any village news they had. Eventually, they would have to resume their journey home. This day, Mary and Hannah walked in communal silence for some time. Suddenly, Mary asked, "How did the well get there, Mommy?"

"We'll ask you father when he gets home," said Hannah. "I am sure he knows."

In a while, Hannah and Mary came to their own home. It was a typical mud-brick home of comfortable four-room design, shoulder to shoulder with the other homes of the neighborhood. They were fortunate to be able to afford plaster on the walls within, and Hannah had decorated them nicely with some modest things she had gotten at the market. Behind, it had a courtyard and a great mulberry tree that offered shade from the rays of the sun.

"Here, Mary, have some water," said Hannah. It was no longer as cold as it was when she got it from the well, but it was a welcome refreshment for their warm, sticky mouths. Hannah said, "It is interesting to think of water to drink as a rainstorm in our mouths. Can you imagine that? Do you remember in the winter when it rained much more than now?"

"The rain comes from the sky," said Mary, remembering.

Next, they had to grind the grain for the day's flatbreads. The grinding stone was in the courtyard, where the shade of the mulberry tree made it the best place to do this work. The tree was finished with its messy berries; they had been good eating earlier in the summer.

"Here, Mary. Take this cup of grain and pour it into this hole here in the center of the grindstone," said Hannah. Mary poured as carefully as she could, but a few corns missed the mark and fell into the rim of the stone race. The two of them carefully picked up each one and put it back into the cup for the next filling.

"Here, Mary. You can help me turn the stone." Hannah grabbed the vertical dowel handle of the grindstone with both hands and turned it around in the race of the counterpart stone. Mary's little hands grabbed confidently the stub of the handle that Hannah ensured would be available for her. The stone turned reasonably easily over the grains but got somewhat harder as they broke down into flour. Eventually, however, the flour was ground enough for making the breads.

"We have to start the fire in the oven," said Hannah. The oven was also in the courtyard. It was a domed earthenware oven in which Hannah built a rack of wood over a kindling of grasses. She went into the house to get the lamp, and brought it out. She took a few stalks of dried grass, lit it from the lamp, and touched it to the kindling. "We won't use charcoal today," she said. "It's too expensive for us to use it every day, even though it's cleaner and hotter to use."

As the fire made the dome hot, Hannah hand-worked the flour with some water and oil into small flat circles and cooked them on the hot surface of the dome, one side and then the other. Today they would cook about a dozen breads. Two or three would be their own midday meal, unless Papa came home. The rest would be for the evening meal.

With the bread done, the ladies went into the house to arrange the midday meal.

"Papa did not say this morning whether he would be home for midday, but as homemakers, we must always be ready, just in case," taught Hannah. Sometimes he would come home at midday, and sometimes not. He would sometimes bring other men, and they would sit on the flat roof of their home, in the shade from the tree in the courtyard, and talk loudly about things the little girl did not yet understand. Hannah went over the items. "The fruits are cleaned and ready, if anyone wants them. Olives are in the fired clay jar, figs in the bowl, flatbreads on the platter on the table. Wine cups are here and the watered wine is in the pottery bottle. Olive oil, salt, and cheese are here. The cucumber can wait."

The little girl had gotten used to her papa being away during the day and Mama being her constant companion. Papa spent a lot of time in the work of the town's House of Prayer. It was modest as houses of prayer went but was, nonetheless, among the more special buildings of this village. Often it had things that needed to be fixed. The Sabbath prayer services required some preparation as well.

Papa did not come home this day at midday. When the little girl realized that he would not be home until later, she felt as though the time would take longer than she wanted. However, she and Mama had enough to do. With Mama leading the way, the day moved along at a pace that was familiar even to Mary.

That evening, Joachim arrived home and greeted his ladies. Hannah gave him a warm glance and returned his greeting.

"Hello, Mary," he said.

"How did the well get there, Papa," Mary asked. She had been waiting all day to ask her question.

Hannah explained how the question became so important to Mary.

Joachim said, "Oh, my, that is a little question, but the answer is very big."

Joachim put her on his lap and explained.

Mary, it is no small task to dig a well, but, if a village is to be able to carry on, the elders have little choice. First, the elders of the village find someone who has done this before. It might be the high priest himself or his helpers. He might even ask someone from another village who has helped dig a well. With the help of these people, the high priest will decide where to dig the well. The day of the digging is fixed by the elders. It is a day of ceremony, speeches, and prayers. It is a day that will live in the memory the village. The digging begins in a very wide area; the workers have to dig out the sides at an angle so that the side of the well does not fall in on them as they are digging. When the hole is so deep that the men cannot throw the dirt up to the edge, they have to haul it up in baskets. Sometimes, they build stairs into the side of the hole. They dig and dig, down and down, until they reach water. Often, they find ancient things, such as animal bones and even human bones. In fact, there is a story that they found a skeleton when they dug this well! Do you know what a skeleton is?

Mary looked wide-eyed at her father and moved her head very slightly to say "No." He continued.

"A skeleton is the bones of a person, or of an animal. We have seen the bones in the meat we roast on Holy Days. We all have bones in our bodies. We have bones in our arms, and our legs. We have bones in our fingers. They give our bodies their shape. When we find them in the ground, we know that a person or an animal died there many years ago."

Mary's little face looked thoughtful, and her mouth pursed as she looked at her own hand.

"You know that animals and people can die," he said gently. "We have seen animals in the fields that got sick, so sick that they could no longer live. That will happen to every living thing."

"Yes," she said quietly. "I know."

He put his arms around her and hugged her warmly. "Ah, my sweet little angel, do not worry. Your mamma and I are here for you and we will keep you safe."

She responded with her little arms around his neck.

"Anyway," he said with renewed enthusiasm, "back to the well."

If the diggers dig a lot and still do not reach water, the elders face a decision. The hole must be made larger at the top and the sides dug out more so that the angle can be preserved, or the project may have to be moved or they may even have to give up.

"That would be a bad thing," said Mary.

"Yes, it would," said her father.

And that is why, when they find water, it is a cause for great joy in the whole village. Then the workers have to set the special stones in the bottom to help filter the water. Layers of gravel will make the water clear. Once the filtration stones are set, the workers build the stone walls from the bottom up. As the wall is set, the dirt is put back around the stonework. The wall and the dirt go in little by little. A larger well brings its own special problems. The walls have to be thicker, the stones larger, the laborers more, the cost higher.

Jaochim stopped his narration and asked Mary, "So, what do you think of that?"

"Will the well be there forever?" she asked.

"It will be there as long as we need it, I am sure," said her father.

However, we do have to take care of it. Sometimes we have to clean the well. This can be dangerous if there is bad air in the well. A worker lowers a lamp to test the safety of the air in the lower parts of the well. If the lamp goes out, the air is not good and the workers must not stay in the well for very long. Even so, the work must be done if the well needs to be cleaned. The workers have to remove all of the water from the well. The villagers will come and take all the water they can, because it will be many days before they can use the well again. Once the well is empty enough, the worker will go in and block off the source of the water. The villagers will watch and stand ready to help if the workers get sick from the bad air. Once the well is cleaned and new filtering stones set in, the water source is reopened. The workers climb out or are lifted out. After some days of waiting to be sure that the well is flushed itself, the people can start using it again.

Mary listened to this story. The mystery of the well changed; she now understood it as a thing of the grown-up world. It came into practical perspective in her mind; it was their source of water. She realized that the grown-ups would take care of it and that she did not have to worry about it anymore.

THE VISITOR

One day, many days later, Joachim said to his wife, "Remember that I am expecting Azach, from Zippori, today, and I will have him with me this evening when I come home. Today I want to work on the House of Prayer and make it especially beautiful for his visit."

"Oh, yes," said Hannah, I remember. I am planning a special meal for your scholar friend. How is his flock in Zippori?"

"Yes. A good rabbi, a good man and a good friend. We have known him for many years," said Joachim. "We really should get together with him more often." Joachim had made his acquaintance years ago on a trip to Jerusalem. Azach favored the Psalms and the moral truths to be gained from them. He and Joachim had discussed Azach's recent plans to go to Jerusalem to study the scriptures, and Azach had agreed to visit Nazareth on his way back to his home. In Zippori and beyond, Azach was a noted speaker and voice of wisdom.

Joachim oversaw a group of volunteers from among the men of the village and their sons, collectively known as the *batlanim*, who attended to the details. A thorough routine cleaning was all it needed. Cleaning of the interior plaster and mural paintings was done the previous year and still looked very nice.

When he first knew that Azach was coming, Joachim told Hannah that Azach would be a guest in their home. Hannah began developing her plans for entertaining this guest. Primarily, they would need to provide him a good meal. They were proud to be able to provide him as well a private place to rest and sleep, since their home had a fourth room.

Hannah and Mary were also busy. The trip to market yesterday had been especially important, so they had taken the one-hour walk to Zippori. There they could find things that were not available in the Nazareth market. They enjoyed the luxury of buying rosemary and cumin, and lamb in honor of the dinner guest. They had also bought more special vegetables and fruits, including fresh almonds, figs, and dates, as well as cucumber, onion, garlic, and chickpeas.

As the afternoon aged, the ladies prepared the food for the evening meal. There was water flavored with lemon to drink, as well as wine, which would be full strength for the meal as opposed to the watered wine that was the usual beverage. There would be flatbread made from the flour and oil bought at the market and cooked on the clay oven. They made olive paste from finely chopped olives, onions, garlic, pepper and salt, and just the right amount of olive oil. It was wonderful on the flatbreads. For their special guest, they had a lamb roast in a covered clay roasting pan inside the oven. They rubbed the roast with salt, pepper, garlic and rosemary. It had about a half-inch of water in it originally, which helped it stay moist through the roasting time. When it was done, the thin, spiced layer of fat would be cooked to a crispy treat, unique in itself. Vegetables included lettuce and fenugreek sprouts with cucumber, vinegar, and olive oil, and a bit of onion. On this summer day, Hannah did not provide a cooked vegetable. After dinner, there would be figs and almonds, cheeses, and additional water or wine.

Soon there was a familiar voice at the front of the house, engaged in conversation.

"Do you hear Papa, Mary?" the mother asked.

Mary answered, "Yes, yes," and, confidently reeling as only three-year-olds can do, ran to the front door, calling to her papa. When she arrived, there was a surprise: a stranger with Papa. She stopped like a jammed saw and stared at the new face.

"Hello, Mary," Papa said cheerfully, picking her up into his arms.

She felt better.

"See, I have brought a friend to have dinner with us. His name is Azach. He lives in Zippori, where you and Mama went to market yesterday. Can you say hello to Azach?"

The child recoiled into Papa's shoulder, but kept the stranger in view out of the corner of her eye. He nonetheless said, "Hello, Mary. I am sure you and I will be good friends in no time. In fact, I have a little girl just about your age. Her name is Rebecca. And, do you know what? She has twenty ribs. I have counted them. I'll show you how I count her ribs."

With that, he gently put his fingers in her ribs and walked them up, counting, "One, two, three…"

The little girl looked at Papa and saw the great smile of fun on his face and, keying off of his lead, could not contain herself. She giggled and squirmed and pushed at the man's hand. He understandingly pulled his hand away. She looked more directly at him, and he put his index finger up by his face and wiggled it in her direction. "I can count your ribs from here, I expect," he said, and she giggled again. Then he put his large hand on her shoulders and patted her, saying, "Ah, you're a blessed man, Joachim."

"Oh, yes, I know, and I thank you, Azach, for saying so," Joachim said. Hannah had arrived near the front door and waited while this scene of fun played out. Joachim invited Azach to enter, and Azach proceeded through the doorway.

"Rabbi Azach of Zippori, you know my wife, Hannah," said Joachim.

"Peace be to this house and to you, Hannah," said Azach.

"Thank you, and peace be to you, Rabbi Azach," said Hannah.

"We shall dine on the roof," said Joachim. "This way."

They proceeded into the house and up the stout ladder-stairway. Joachim offered his guest a rustic but sturdy seat at an equally modest table. The sun moved towards the horizon on this sixth day of the week. The shadows grew longer and fainter as the moment of the Sabbath grew near.

Instinctively, as it had for innumerable years, the ear of the village was listening for the sound of the Shofar from the House of Prayer. All talk stops and all ears listen to hear the familiar pattern: one blast, a pause for breath, and then the second blast, of such a length that people were impressed with Levi's ability, even after so many years. Everyone knew that now all work must stop. But they still would wait for the last sound, more faint than the others, showing that the herald had carried the Shofar to its resting place before the final tone and had not offended the Sabbath by carrying it after it was sounded. Now also the Sabbath-lamp was lit, indicating the feast day had begun.

The meal, which the ladies prepared before sundown, was ready for them. It required no additional preparation. The flatbread was ready for dipping in the olive paste. Watermelon was cut into small wedges that only required one bite at the end and did not require any breaking of the rind. Joachim and Hannah had discussed this over the years and decided on this approach for the Sabbath because it was a reasonable way to observe the Sabbath rest. The flatbread was torn into similar wedges for a similar reason. Even the roast was cut to bite-sized pieces to minimize the actions needed to eat the meal.

The men sat at the table. Azach told Joachim that he would enjoy it if Hannah and Mary joined them at the table. He was very willing to offer a blessing for the food when Joachim asked him. Inspired by the little child in front of him, he spoke the words of a loving son of the most high.

> *Father of all,*
> *We, your children, turn our hearts to you.*
> *We offer you what we can:*
> *our devotion in every waking moment,*
> *and holy courage in the face of every challenge.*
> *We bring to you our tininess,*
> *our limited abilities,*
> *and beg you for completion.*
> *We thank you for the joys of this life,*

for this lovely family
and this table of food,
the blessings of your earth.
We shall enjoy it in the spirit
of your loving care.

They quietly contemplated these thoughts. Joachim said, "Thank you, Azach. That was beautifully made."

They began their meal. Joachim said, "So, tell me of your travels, Azach. What villages have you been to?"

Well, on this journey, I went straight to Jerusalem for study of the Proverbs and of the Prophets. I am always seeking to refine my understanding of what the Father wants of us, that is, each of us, as one of his people. For all of us, the rules are the same, but for each of us, the application of those rules is special. I don't think we look into that very much. However, I planned to visit a few villages on my way back home in order to share what I learned with the people there. I have been to Ephraim, Neapolis, Salim, and Nain, and now I am here a few steps from my own home sharing my thoughts. It is so generous of you to invite me. Apparently, the word has spread about how much I enjoy speaking to the people about the wisdom of the scriptures.

Joachim said, "The word has spread about how captivating your message is." Joachim was very pleased to have this noted scholar as a friend and as a guest in the Nazareth House of Prayer. He felt a sense of camaraderie and professionalism in this friend.

Joachim then asked, "In Nain, Jacob is the Archisynagogos there, is he not? How is he doing?"

Azach answered, "He is well. His people are somewhat involved in open hostility with the Romans, but he is keeping the lid on pretty well."

"Oh, I hate to see that. The hostility, I mean. I do not see much future in wrestling with the Romans," said Joachim. After a quiet moment, he said, "So, Azach, how is the life of the Temple going in Jerusalem?"

"It was quite strong and vibrant, considering our political situation," he said. "On the Sabbath last, there was a very elaborate service, with choral and instrumental music. It was as if we had been by the throne of heaven itself." Their discussion went on into the night, and finally the household retired. Tomorrow, Azach would attend the Sabbath service and listen to the sermon of Rabbi Jacob. Then Joachim and Rabbi Jacob would leisurely escort Azach home and return to Nazareth.

GROWING

Hannah's circle of friends was most supportive of her being an older new mother. She picked up the patterns of the younger mothers. They would watch each other's children when urgent matters came up, and these children came to know the others in their own generation, those with whom they would mature and grow old. This is how Mary grew closer to the other children in the village. Village life was as pleasant as one could ask for young Mary.

At that time, Mary's acquaintances were both boys and girls. In the years to come, that would change as boys went to school and apprenticed with their fathers or other mentors in the village. Mary's world would be composed of women acting in their well-defined roles or of girls learning those roles.

In the time between five and eight years of age, Mary developed a confident interest in the parts of the village she knew. Hannah would tell her the names of her neighbors, and they would visit as occasions arose.

"Mary, today we are going to visit Rachel, the widow, who lives two houses away. She is blessed to have a good son who can care for her in her older days."

"Shall we take her a bowl of chick-peas? Last time we gave her some cucumbers, I remember," said Mary.

"I think chick-peas are a good idea," said Hannah.

"She always treats us so nicely," said Mary.

They readied the chick-peas in a modest pottery bowl with a matching cover and walked to Rachael's son's home. They called out their hellos and were greeted by Rachael's daughter-in-law.

"Hello, Miriam," said Hannah.

"Oh, hello, Hannah. Hello, Mary. How are you," said Miriam with a genuine smile.

"We are here to visit you and Rachael. Is she in," asked Hannah.

"Oh, certainly. Come in. We were just preparing the evening meal."

They entered the humble house and saw Rachael sitting at the handmade table in the kitchen. Her little frame was bent forward and she leaned on the table only half-awake.

"Someone is here to see you, Mama," said Miriam. As soon as Rachael saw Mary and Hannah, she became a different person, and cried out "Ooh, hello, hello, hello! Oh, come and see me my dear Mary." She remained at the table, but extended her arms. Mary entered the embrace and gave Rachael's small bony frame a return hug.

A hand-hewn bench was available for the women to sit on. They sat down and the exchange of news and pleasantries went on. Rachel would dote on Mary. She had no daughter of her own and loved her friendship with this young girl. She always kept a sweet date in supply in case Mary would visit. It made Mary feel somewhat gown up to have this elderly woman consider her a special friend.

"Here Rachael, we brought you a little gift," said Hannah, as Mary held out for her the little bowl of chick-peas.

Rachael responded, "Oh, you sweet dears. You bring joy to an old lady." Rachel got up from her throne in this tiny one-house realm, and went to the counter where she had her special gift for Mary.

"I have something for you, too," she said, and offered her simple gift.

Mary took the date, and said a genuine, heartfelt "Thank you." They discussed more things and, eventually, the time for parting arrived. They all stood and shared embraces around. Mary and Hannah wended their way home to complete another of their allotted days in the village.

As the years passed by, the routine of daily life the village was segmented by the recreative power of Holy Day breaks. Holy Days would see extended families and communities gather to share in the worship of the special day, in feasting, relaxing, and catching up on family and community news. There was also an extended family for Mary. As the feast of Pentecost arrived the year Mary was about ten, she and her parents went to the home of Hannah's nephew, Jonathan, and his wife, Rivka. They had a sheep herd out by the edge of the village.

As they walked, Mary asked her father, "What are all the Holy Days we have? I know we have many all year long, but I don't know them all."

Joachim was very pleased when his daughter asked such questions. It gave him a chance to inform the mind of this child and to talk about his favorite subject: the religious culture he loved. Thus, he began.

"We have many Holy Days throughout the year. We keep track of the year with a calendar, and the calendar is based on three things: the days as they go on one by one; the changing of the moon, month by month, and the years. The yearly calendar, first of all, contains twelve months."

He explained them carefully and had Mary repeat them.

"The month of Nisan is thirty days long. Say that."

Mary repeated his words dutifully.

"Iyar is twenty-nine days," he said. Mary repeated. On they went.

Sivan is thirty days; Tammuz is twenty-nine days; Av is thirty days; Elul, twenty-nine; Tishrei, thirty; Cheshvan can be twenty-nine or thirty days long; Kislev twenty-nine or thirty days; Tevet, twenty-nine days; and Shevat, thirty days. Adar is twenty-nine days.

"How do we know when a month begins?" asked Mary. Her father explained.

Each month begins when the first bit of the moon appears after the moon is all dark. When there is a new moon, we tell the Sanhedrin. They are the men who help us run our village. When they hear testimony from two good witnesses about what day the new moon appears, they declare the rosh chodesh and send out messengers to tell people when the month began. Of course, we can see the moon as well and can usually tell when the new month begins.

But, you know, there is something interesting about the calendar. We know that the calendar does not keep up with the sun and the moon exactly. Somehow, we don't know exactly how, the months get earlier each year. So, we use a twelve-month calendar most of the time, and we let it go for two or three years. Then we add an extra month of Adar. That brings things back to fit with the moon's cycle.

"That's pretty clever," said Mary. After a little thought, she asked,

"How do we decide whether the extra month should be added?"

"Bright girl," her father thought to himself, and he went on.

The Sanhedrin observes the weather, the crops and the livestock. If these do not show that spring is near, the Sanhedrin orders the extra month to be put in. The main thing we need is to be very sure that Passover is in the spring.

"Now, Nissan—say Nissan," he bade her.

"Nissan," said her sweet voice.

He could not help but smile. "Nissan contains the Holy Day Passover. Passover celebrates the life of Moses."

"I know Moses," she said. "His mama put him in the river in a basket."

"Yes," said her father.

He was orphaned as a baby and set adrift in the river by his poor Jewish mother, a slave in Egypt. He was found by the daughter of the king in Egypt and she took him as her own child. He grew up in the court of the king and became a leader in Egypt. But when he was grown, he got into some trouble and had to move far away to live. Then God made him the leader of Israel's struggle to be free of slavery. God worked great miracles through Moses and freed His people from their bondage to the Egyptian Pharaoh, using Moses.

Now, Iyar contains what we call the Second Passover and Lag b'Omer.

"I've heard of that," Mary said, "but I don't remember what it is." Her father went on happily.

Leviticus tells us to count seven complete weeks from the day after Passover night. The thirty-third day of the counting of the Omer is Lag b'Omer. The end of the seven weeks is the festival of Shavuot on the fiftieth day. The forty-nine days of the Omer correspond both to the time between freedom from Egypt and the spiritual freedom we got when God gave Moses the Torah at the foot of Mount Sinai on Shavuot. This time also is the time between the barley harvest and the wheat harvest.

Sivan is the month that contains the Shavuot Holy Day. It is one of the three Biblical pilgrimage festivals that we are to keep as we are told in the book of Exodus. I could go into that detail, but I won't right now.

"How many more are there," Mary asked, her interest beginning to wane.

"Oh, there are quite a few," he answered. "Shall I go on?"

"Yes," she answered, knowing that this was important information she was hearing. Besides, they still had a good long walk to make before they would get to cousin Jonathan's house.

"Very good," he said.

Tammuz is the next month, and it contains the fast day we call the Seventeenth of Tammuz. The Babylonian armies of King Nebuchadnezzar broke through the walls of Jerusalem on the ninth of Tammuz nearly five hundred years ago. King Ziddikiahu, or Zedekiah, of Judah, was captured and taken to Babylon. For a month, the armies destroyed one building after another in Jerusalem, including the Holy Temple. They took most of our people to Babylon, and made slaves of us. For many years since then, we have celebrated the memory of Tammuz nine. But, only about seventy years ago, the Romans broke the walls of Jerusalem on the seventeenth of Tammuz, so now we have the fast day on the seventeenth.

He looked at her, and she looked at him. "Shall I go on," he asked.

She wagged her head with big eyes and said, in jest, "My mind is filling up." But she knew it was important, and she did want to know, so she said, "Yes, go on, Papa."

Very well. Av contains the fast day Tishah B'av, when we fast to remember the mistake our forefathers made in complaining to Moses. They were afraid of the danger of moving into Canaan.

For their lack of faith in God, their generation was required then to wander in the desert for forty years.

The month of Elul is a time of repentance in preparation for the High Holy Days of Rosh Hashanah and Yom Kippur. The word "Elul" means "search." Elul is a time to search one's heart and draw close to God in preparation for the coming Day of Judgment, Rosh Hashanah, and Day of Atonement, Yom Kippur.

Tishrei, contains Rosh Hashanah, the fast of Gedaliah, Yom Kippur, and Sukkot. Rosh Hashanah is the Feast of the Trumpets referred to in the book of Leviticus, where it tells us that in the seventh month, in the first day of the month, we must have a sabbath, a memorial of blowing of trumpets and a holy convocation. We are to do no servile work, but are to make an offering by fire unto the Lord. So that is the feast of the Trumpets.

Gedaliah was a governor in Juda appointed by Nebuchadnezzar. He urged the people to plant and to have hope, and they prospered. Later, he was killed by a bad person. The day of death was the ending of the First Jewish nation, so it is a day of fasting and repentance.

Yom Kippur, the Feast of Atonement, is on the tenth day of Tishri. It is a special fast. The main reason for the day is to think about the community sins and personal sins of the whole year. We honestly confront them as sins and atone for them to God. On this day, the high priest makes confession of all the sins of the community and enters on their behalf into the most holy place. He takes with him the blood of reconciliation. It is a very holy time when the people, through true sorrow for sin, offer themselves to God's mercy. He gives us His forgiveness. It makes us very glad before Him, and we renew our promises to carry out His commandments.

"I'm confused now," Mary said. "I'm sorry, Papa."

"I know it is a lot," he said. "Let me finish and you do your best to remember. We will repeat this, I am sure, many other times, too."

He continued, and Mary recommitted her attention.

The feast of Tabernacles, or Sukkoth, is in the book of Leviticus also, where it says that on the fifteenth day of the seventh month, when we have gathered in the fruit of the land, we shall keep a feast for seven days. On the first day there shall be a Sabbath-rest, and on the eighth day a Sabbath-rest. On the first day, we take the fruit of beautiful trees, branches of palm trees, the boughs of leafy trees and willows of the brook, and rejoice before our God. The law tells us that all who are native Israelites shall dwell in booths, that the people will know forever that God made the children of Israel dwell in booths when He brought them out of the land of Egypt.

The next month is Marcheshvan, *commonly known as Cheshvan. It doesn't have any Holy Days in it. Isn't that interesting?*

Mary made a silent nod of her head, agreeing, if somewhat dutifully, that it was indeed interesting.

Kislev contains Chanukah. This festival was started by Judah Maccabee. The terrible King Antiochus IV had persecuted us and ruined our Temple. Judah led our people in a long fight with Antiochus's armies. Finally, he won for us the right to worship. After recovering Jerusalem and the Temple, Judah ordered the Temple to be cleansed, a new altar to be built in place of the polluted one, and new holy vessels to be made.

Now, you know that we burn the Menorah in the Temple throughout the night every night. It takes eight days to prepare olive oil for the Menorah. But, at that time, there was only enough oil to burn for one day. Yet, the Menorah burned for eight days. So, we have this festival, Chanukah, to remember that great miracle.

Tevet is the next month. One thing that happened in the month of Tevet was that Ezra, the Scribe, died on the ninth of Tevet. He was a great leader who brought the Jews back to the holy land from the Babylonian exile and who ushered in the era of the Second Temple.

So, Tevet contains the fast day the tenth of Tevet. This fast makes us remember many things that have happened throughout our history about this time. For example, on the eighth of Tevet, about two hundred years ago, there was Hellenistic rule in Judea. Ptolemy was the King of Egypt. He ordered the translation of our scriptures into Greek. He put seventy sages into solitary confinement and ordered them each to translate the Torah into Greek. Ptolemy expected that the outcome would be a whole bunch of different translations and that the holiness of the Torah would be shaken by that. But, listen! All seventy sages independently made the exact same translations into Greek. The Greeks were amazed.

"That was a great thing," said Mary.

The next month, Shevat, contains Tu Bishvat, which we call the New Year for Trees. You know that we may not eat the fruit of a tree for the first three years of its life, and the fourth year's fruit we must bring to the Temple. The counting of the ritual years begins on Tu Bishvat.

Adar contains the fast of Esther and the Holy Day of Purim. We remember the way Esther and Moredcai were used by God to thwart the plan of Haman under King Ahasuerus to wipe out our people, and how Purim, the day of celebration for that deliverance, was proclaimed.

And that's the way the year is set up. You're a good girl to listen to that long story. I am so proud of you for wanting to know these things.

Again, in her fashion, Mary was thinking silently. Finally, she said.

"There are a lot of things that God has done for us," she answered. "It's good to remember them. I hope I can."

"Your knowledge will grow stronger each time we explain these things to you. Every year, we will celebrate these Holy Days, and their meaning will be clearer each time you see them. It makes me very happy that you enjoy learning these things," he said.

They walked on and talked of these things more, but soon they were at the house of Jonathan, Hannah's nephew, and Rivka, his wife.

Rivka had a number of brothers, and they were also at most of the Holy Day gatherings with their families. Here they renewed old family ties and stretched them to new dimensions. In some cases, old animosities were put aside for a while. In this extended family, as in all others, kin of all kinds, like Mary and her cousin, living at widely separated points, could see what a salad-like mixture of personalities, experiences, and values they were. There too, they would have the corners of their personal quirks smoothed off, if only slightly. In the background, always, was the benign influence of their common faith in the Lord.

The children went off to play or talk, depending on their ages, and unconsciously observe the changes in their minds and bodies, from loose teeth to comparing height to sharing worldly wisdom that they had learned since they last met. Season to season, these experiences would tumble with the rules and wisdom received from their elders. After the feast days, the children would bring their subtle changes home to their familiar environments, adopt ever so slightly new ways of acting and thinking, and form slightly new attitudes about themselves and their lives. In these incremental stages of growing, personalities took shape, choices were made, and the children grew closer, or further, from a true internal relationship with God.

Separately, the men gathered and talked of the events of their lives. They saw themselves as fighting the Lord's battles in their own particular ways. Mary and the other children would hear their loud, unguarded discussions and get glimpses of the diverse elements of life in their place and time, from politics to religion, farming to business, wealth to poverty, health to sickness: in sum, all aspects of survival and death as it unfolded in the village and beyond.

This day, Mary hovered closer to where the men were talking. She was especially curious to hear these views of the adult world. Roman influence in this area, only four miles from the Roman city of Zippori, was firm.

"Did you hear that Octavian is now calling himself 'Emperor Caesar Augustus,' of all things," one of them said. "Some twenty years ago, he was just a war lord, when he defeated Anthony."

"Yeah," said another, "when that poser Herod claimed the Jewish throne in Jerusalem." The people had no love for him.

"He's just a gentile who pretended to adopt our faith; there was no sincerity when he and his family 'became' Jews," said a third.

"He thinks we are fooled by his marrying a princess of the Hasmonean Dynasty. He clothes himself in the heroism of Judas the Maccabee, and his brother, Simon."

"They won four victories over occupying armies and purified and rededicated the Temple in Jerusalem. They also won independence for Judah and established the Dynasty, fighting against Herod's kind. But that was a hundred years ago. There is no glory in it any more."

"I heard that Herod actually worshipped Augustus in Rome. He's just a charlatan, a puppet. He's in tight with Rome now, but just wait until he makes a mistake."

"Well, he has done some remarkable things," said one. He's rebuilt the Temple. You have to say it is very beautiful."

"Yes, and he actually moved the City of Jericho. It is further south now, and he brought water-channels to the city. I can't imagine how anyone could have the power to do something like that."

"Yes, but he still is not friend to God. He built himself a great palace there with our money. He's also built a grand Hellenistic theater," said one, with a distasteful tone of voice.

Whatever that was, it did not sound good to Mary. It stressed Mary to learn also that people had different ideas about God. The Sadducees were rich people, and they believed in doing only what the writings exactly said. They were willing to work with the Roman leaders. There were some businessmen who, by their roles, tended to be in the group of the Sadducees. The Pharisees were the common people. They were rabbis who thought that the law needed to be explained and added details in writing to the Torah. They did not want anything to do with Roman leaders. There were other groups like the Essenes, who chose to live very poor lives and only think about God. There were also the Zealots, who felt that there must be fighting to make the Romans leave and allow Israel to be in charge of its own land.

As Mary listened to the men talk, one of them noticed her and chided her, "What are you doing here, girl? You've got no business here. Go on, now. Go off with the women."

Mary was chagrinned by the comment, even though it was expected that young women not busy themselves with men's concerns. Being now about twelve, Mary found herself with a profound interest in these things. She processed everything she overheard in the marketplace, in the streets of the village, and in the family Holy Day gatherings. She did not discuss them much with the other children, but just found them to be what her mind would constantly return to and tumble over and over. She tried to fit them together, like pieces of a giant mental puzzle. It bothered her greatly that the pieces never seemed to fit together well.

THE HOUSE OF PRAYER

After some years, the chance arose for Joachim to invite his old friend, Rabbi Azach of Zippori, to address the Nazareth community at the Sabbath worship. Joachim again was eager to prepare the building especially well for this visit.

While Joachim had been to Jerusalem and seen the Temple a number of times, he always enjoyed talking with anyone who had recently been there. Their faith considered only the Temple in Jerusalem to be its temple, and all other places of worship to be community houses. The Nazareth House was called *Beit Tefila* (House of Prayer) instead of *Beit Knesset* (House of Assembly) as some of the houses in Zippori were called.

A community would build its own House of Prayer, sometimes with the charitable assistance of neighbors or of private donations. If this failed, the community might meet for worship in a private dwelling, a sort of "synagogue in a house." In worship services, the learned and the ignorant strove together to understand the Scriptures. The villagers would worship together, but nonetheless take their places in recognition of their earthly rank, with leaders sitting with the elders and other honored persons towards the front and the more humble men towards the back.

When Azach arrived for this visit, their friendship took up as if they had not been apart. They discussed their plans for the Sabbath address and of the local House of Prayer.

"I know that you have many batlanim to prepare this House of Prayer for the Sabbath worship," Azach said. "It is a tribute to your leadership."

Jewish tradition expected that a House of Prayer be staffed by ten men of leisure, batlanim, or volunteers, who would devote their time to the House of Prayer, to the study of the Torah, and to the other community programs provided there.

Joachim said, "You are generous, Azach. We have been blessed of course for many generations with holy men who have devoted much of their lives to this work."

Houses of Prayer were not used only for prayer, but also for adult and child education and community activities. Thus, most had a main sanctuary for prayer and smaller rooms for study. Rooms set aside for study are referred to as beth midrash (house of study).

The structure of the Sabbath worship resulted in the buildings having similar major features. However, there was room for artistic creativity from one community to the next. Paintings and ornamentation within did not include sculpture or general natural objects, out of a concern for avoiding idolatry. However, some symbols were viewed as proper, such as the interlaced triangles, the lion of Judah, and flower and fruit forms. Occasionally the shofar, and even the lulab or lulav, was used in the design. The lulab is the festive palm branch, which, with the etrog, the good fruit of a godly tree, often a citron, is described in Leviticus, Chapter 23.

. …and you shall take of yourselves on the first day [of Sukkot] the fruit of a goodly tree, a palm branch, the myrtle branch, and the willow of the brook; and you shall rejoice before the Lord your God seven days.

"In some areas, prayer towards the east was condemned, on the ground of the false worship of the rising sun towards the east mentioned in Ezekiel, chapter 8, verse 16. In other places, the advice is simply given to turn towards Jerusalem, in whatever direction it be. In general, however, it was considered that since the presence of God, or Shekhinah, was everywhere in Palestine, direction was not of much importance."

Joachim enjoyed showing the House of Prayer to his friend.

"Azach," he said, "we believe that Nazareth's House of Prayer dates back to the Babylonian captivity. The roof is flat, with the columns connected by blocks of stone on which massive rafters rest. The walls are two or more feet thick, and built of local field stones. As you see, the building has a good number of windows to admit light. And it is rough on the exterior, but the inside is plastered smooth and frescoed with symbols of our faith."

Azach said, "I love the design of this House. The murals are rich reminders of the great events Israel's history. Here is the menorah on the lintel, here an open flower between two Paschal lambs, here are vine-leaves and grapes, a bowl of manna with Aaron's rod. It is inspiring."

Joachim said, "It is, of course, not for us to know every date when improvements have been made, but it is today very well appointed. The floor, for example, is white limestone, but we do not know if it is original. The double colonnades are more likely original, since they are fundamental to the construction of the building."

"Yes, yes," agreed Azach.

The aisles east and west of the colonnade were the passages. The distance between the columns was but nine or ten feet. The two corner columns at the northern end had their two exterior faces square like pillars, and the two interior ones were formed by half-engaged pillars. In front of these pillars was the women's gallery.

Joachim pointed out the features of the worship hall. "We think that the Ark is beautiful with this ornate curtain outside the Ark doors. And here is the constant light as a reminder of the constantly lit menorah of the Temple in Jerusalem. This large, elevated reader's platform suits the importance of the reading of the Torah. We use a pulpit instead of a desk for the delivery of the sermon. Our pulpit is not placed on either side of the Ark, but is right here in the center of the steps. It is readily designed so that we can carry it outside in the streets on public fasts.

"Here, right before the Ark, and facing the people, are the seats for the leaders of the House of Prayer and other honorable persons. You will sit here.

"The Sanhedrin is not convened this week. There are no legal matters to bring before it now. So, how does this compare to the Temple in Jerusalem?"

Azach answered, "As you know, there are strict rules for the Temple in Jerusalem. You cannot carry a staff into it, nor wear shoes, nor even have any dust on your feet. Also you cannot have any money or purse with you."

"Yes, I know of these rules," said Joachim. "However, a synagogue or House of Prayer, by comparison, is considered not so holy a space, and these rules do not pertain to them in the same way. Even so, a House of Prayer does require serious attention to respectful behavior, as shown by the rules against using it as a shortcut, against joking, laughter, eating, talking, or putting on or removing coats or similar concerns."

Joachim added, smiling, "You know that no one should go in just for shelter from the sun or rain. But we have many holy visitors on hot afternoons."

Azach spoke up of his experience.

Of course, our rabbi and his disciple, as is expected, look upon the building as if it were their own dwelling. Still, it is very rarely that we see them eat, drink, or perhaps even sleep in the building. On some emergency occasions, we have housed some poor strangers here, but in general, we treat it as the building consecrated to God that it is.

Money collected for the building may be used for other purposes, but things dedicated to the Temple cannot be sold. A synagogue may be converted into an academy, because the latter is regarded as more sacred than a synagogue, but not vice versa. Village synagogues may be disposed of, under the direction of the local Sanhedrin, but it cannot afterward be used for such things as public baths, a wash-house, or a tannery. But town synagogues cannot be sold because strangers may have contributed to them; and they have a right to look for some place of worship.

"But I have carried on," Azach said. "Your House of Prayer is ready to meet the Sabbath as a bride or a queen. It is beautiful."

"I love to make it splendid," said Joachim. "Especially for a distinguished visitor."

Both men knew without saying that on the Friday before the Sabbath, the preparatory work is done, including lighting the Sabbath lamp. It gave them comfort to consider how, in their homes, the faithful dressed to suit the Sabbath and provided the table with the best things the family could afford. Also, there was the qiddush, or benediction, spoken over the cup of wine, which, as always, was mixed with water. As Sabbath morning broke, they hastened with quick steps to the synagogue, for such was the rabbinic rule in going. On the other hand, it was prescribed to return home with slow and lingering steps.

THE SABBATH

Mary asked her father about the Sabbath worship. "I know it comes to us from Moses, in Numbers, and Deuteronomy, but I want to know more," she said.

He began his answer. "Well," he said, "I have seen many a Sabbath ceremony. It is a beautiful and complete reminder of our history with God."

One thing to know is the ministers for it. The lowest of these is the Chazzan, or minister, who often acts also as schoolmaster. Often he will conduct the services. Despite his lower ranking, we choose him with great care. He and his family must be true examples for the community. He must have humility, modesty, and knowledge of the Scriptures. He must speak very clearly so that the people can hear him and understand him. He must dress simply and neatly, and he must be free of pride. He must deal politely and kindly with other people.

Mary said, "Jacob the baker is that one, isn't he? They live four houses up from us."

"That's right, my dear. Can you say 'Chazzan'?" he asked her.

Mary carefully repeated the term to her father. He then went on.

"Above the ministers are the elders or Zeqenim. They are also called rulers and sometimes called 'shepherds.' The chief of this group is the Archisynagogos."

"That's a big word," Mary said, "but I have heard it before."

Yes. It means that he is the leader of the synagogue. But, we must remember that he is only the first among his equals. Every ruler of the synagogue is examined as to his knowledge and, if he is acceptable, is ordained to the office. They also form the local Sanhedrin or tribunal. However, they are elected by the congregation, who consider many traits such as absence of pride, and the presence of gentleness and humility.

In some places or times, there are some unordained elders. They only have charge of outward affairs, and act rather as a committee of managers. The elders set the form for the divine service, and determine who is called up to read from the Law and the Prophets, who will conduct the prayers, who will act as Sheliach Tsibbur (messenger of the congregation), and who, if anyone, will deliver an address. That is what Azach will do tomorrow.

"It will be nice to hear him. I like to listen to him when he visits our house," said Mary.

Her father went on.

The Archisynagogos also sees to it that nothing improper takes place in the synagogue, and that the prayers are properly conducted. He is very careful that both the service and the building are properly taken care of.

The reader of the scriptures will go to the Bima. You know what the Bima is, right?

"Yes," she said. "It's right in front of the Ark."

"That's right," he said to her. "That's very good."

Well then, the reader stands at the lectern, and begins the service with two prayers. The first one is this.

'Blessed be You, O Lord, King of the world, Who form the light and create the darkness, Who make peace, and create every thing; Who, in mercy, give light to the earth, and to those who dwell upon it, and in Your goodness, day by day, and every day, renew the works of creation. Blessed be the Lord our God for the glory of His handiworks, and for the light-giving lights which He has made for His praise. Selah. Blessed be the Lord our God, Who has formed the lights.'

"Isn't that a beautiful prayer?" he asked her. She looked at him and nodded agreement. He went on.

The next one is this.

'With great love have You loved us, O Lord our God, and with much overflowing pity have You pitied us, our Father and our King. For the sake of our fathers who trusted in You, and You taught them the statutes of life, have mercy upon us, and teach us. Enlighten our eyes in Your Law; cause our hearts to cleave to Your commandments; unite our hearts to love and fear Your Name, and we shall not be put to shame, world without end. For You are a God Who preparest salvation, and us hast You chosen from among all nations and tongues, and hast in truth brought us near to Your great Name—Selah—that we may lovingly praise You and Your Unity. Blessed be the Lord, Who in love chose His people Israel.'

'True it is that You are Y-W-H, our God, and the God of our fathers, our King, and the King of our fathers, our Savior, and the Savior of our fathers, our Creator, the Rock of our Salvation, our Help and our Deliverer. Your Name is from everlasting, and there is no God beside You. A new song did they that were delivered sing to Your Name by the seashore; together did all praise and own You King, and say, Jehovah shall reign, world without end! Blessed be the God Who saveth Israel.'

After this comes the Shema, asking the people to hear what God wants of them. It is three passages from the Torah. The first one tells us to love God, learn the Torah, and pass on our traditions to our children.

The second paragraph speaks about the blessings of obeying God and the troubles that we have when we do not. The third paragraph speaks about the command to wear the tzitzit, in order to remember our escape from Egypt and the commands Moses received then. The tzitzit remind us of the 613 commandments in the Torah. The word "tzitzit" means "six hundred." That number, plus the five knots and eight strings on each corner, add up to 613. When this prayer is finished, the leader of the ceremony takes his place before the Ark, and there repeats certain 'Eulogies' or Benedictions. There are nineteen of them and they date from different periods. On Sabbaths, only the three first and the three last of them, which are also the oldest, are repeated. Between them, certain other prayers inserted The first Benediction is said with bent body. It is this.

'Blessed be the Lord our God, and the God of our fathers, the God of Abraham, and the God of Isaac, and the God of Jacob; the Great, the Mighty, and the Terrible God, the Most High God, Who shows mercy and kindness. Who creates all things, Who remembers the gracious promises to the fathers, and brings a Savior to their children's children, for His own Name's sake, in love. O King, Helper, Savior, and Shield! Blessed are Thou, O Jehovah, the Shield of Abraham.'

Then there is this.

'You, O Lord, are mighty forever; You, Who quicken the dead, are mighty to save. In Your mercy You preserve the living, You quicken the dead; in Your abundant pity You bear up those who fall, and heal those who are diseased, and loosen those who are bound, and fulfill Your faithful word to those who sleep in the dust. Who is like unto You, Lord of strength, and who can be compared to You, Who kill and make alive, and cause salvation to spring forth? And faithful are You to give life to the dead. Blessed are You, Jehovah, Who quicken the dead!'

Then there is this.

'You are Holy, and Your name is Holy. Selah. Blessed are You Jehovah God, the Holy One.'

Then come the concluding Eulogies, which are these.

'Take gracious pleasure, O Jehovah our God, in Your people Israel and in their prayers, and in love accept the burnt offerings of Israel, and their prayers with Your good pleasure, and may the services of Your people be ever acceptable unto You. And O that our eyes may see it, as You turnest in mercy to Zion. Blessed be Thou, O Jehovah, Who restoreth His Shekhinah to Zion.'

In saying the next Eulogy, which was simply one of thanks, all should bend down. It is this.

'We give praise to You, because You are He, Jehovah, our God, and the God of our fathers, forever and ever. The Rock of our life, the Shield of our salvation, You are He, from generation to generation. We laud You, and declare Your praise. For our lives which are bound up in Thine Hand, for our souls which are committed to You, and for Your wonders which are with us every day and for Your marvelous deeds and Your goodnesses which are at all seasons, evening, and morning, and midday—You Gracious One, for Your compassions never end, You Pitying One, for Your mercies never *cease, forever do we put our trust in You. And for all this, blessed and exalted be Your Name, our King, always, world without end. And all the living bless You—Selah—and praise Your Name in truth, O God, our Salvation and our Help. Selah. Blessed are Thou, Jehovah. The Gracious One is Your Name, and to You it is pleasant to give praise.'*

> *After this, the priests, if any are in the House, speak the blessing, elevating their hands up to the shoulders. In the Temple in Jerusalem, they raise their hands above their heads. This is called the lifting up of hands. In the synagogue, the priestly blessing is in three sections, and the people each time respond by an 'Amen.' Lastly, in the House of Payer, the word 'Adonai' is used instead of Jehovah. If no descendants of Aaron are present, the leader of the devotions says the priestly benediction. After the benediction comes the last Eulogy, which is this.*

'O bestow on Your people Israel great peace forever. For You are King, and Lord of all peace. And it is good in Thine eyes to bless Your people Israel at all times and at every hour with Your peace. Blessed are Thou, Jehovah, Who blesseth His people Israel with peace!'

> *Some rabbis add at the close of this Eulogy certain prayers of their own, either fixed or free. There are some set out in the Talmud. If the priest is a descendant of Aaron, before pronouncing the blessing, he may put off his shoes. In the benediction, the priests turn towards the people, while he who led the ordinary prayers stands with his back to the people, looking towards the Sanctuary. They who pronounce the benediction must have no blemish on their hands, face, or feet, so as not to attract attention. This is especially true in the Temple. Strict sobriety must be shown on such occasions. The public prayers closes with an 'Amen', spoken by the congregation.*

This ends the liturgical part of the service. At this time, the primary object of the service begins, the reading of the Law. The reading of the Law is preceded and followed by brief Benedictions. The Chazzan, or minister, approaches the Ark, and brings out a roll of the Law. It is taken from its case, the têq or teqah, and unwound from those cloths, or the mitpachoth, which holds it. On the Sabbath, at least seven persons are called upon successively to read portions from the Law. None of the readings will consist of less than three verses. On the 'days of congregation,' that is, the third and sixth days, three persons are called up; on New Moon's Day, and on the intermediate days of a festive week, four; on feast days, five; and on the Day of Atonement, six. These are set out in a pattern so that all of the Pentateuch gets read over the course of a little over three years. But, around certain festive days, the ordinary readings are replaced with portions that bear on the feast itself. As the Talmud requires, a descendant of Aaron is always called up first for the reading; then follows a Levite, and afterwards five ordinary Israelites.

After the Law follows a section from the Prophets, what we call the Haphtarah. These are in Hebrew, which many of us do not understand, so we have the Methurgeman, or Interpreter, who stands by the side of the reader, and translates it for us. The Methurgeman is not allowed to read his translation, because the people may think that his words are authoritative. So long as the substance of the text is given correctly, the Methurgeman might paraphrase for better popular understanding.

The reading of the section from the Prophets is followed by a sermon, called the Derashah, that is, where a rabbi capable of giving such instruction or a distinguished visitor is present. We trace the work of preaching back to Moses, who told us that, on the various festivals, we should explain the rites and require the people to perform them.

The preacher needs to be mentally and morally qualified. We know that Azach is a very good man, don't we?

Mary nodded "yes."

Now a great rabbi may employ a Methurgeman to explain to the people his sermon. Of course, he selects him carefully for the purpose. Such an interpreter is also called Amora, or speaker. Perhaps the rabbi would whisper to him his remarks, while he would repeat them aloud; or else he would only condescend to give hints, which the Amora would amplify; or he would speak in Hebrew, and the Amora translate it into Aramæan, Greek, Latin, or whatever the language of the people might be, for the sermon must reach the people in their own tongue.

The Methurgeman also, at the close of the sermon, answers questions or meets objections. If the preacher is a very great man, he may employ one of his students to speak to the Amora. This is also what we do when the preacher is in mourning for a very near relative. Note that, even then, his preaching is so important that it must not be interrupted, even by his personal sorrows or the religious obligations of mourning. Preaching is a most important function. It glorifies God, and brings men nearer to Him; it quenches the soul's thirst. A preacher is like the deliverer of a little city, weak and besieged. The Divine Spirit rests on him, and his office confers as much merit on him as if he had offered both the blood and the fat upon the altar of burnt offering. Mary listened with surprising interest for a young daughter of Israel.

She seemed to appreciate each element of the ritual.

"What do think," asked her father.

"It is a beautiful way He cares for us," she said.

“Young woman, you amaze me,” said her father. She simply smiled in return.

AZACH'S SERMON

The Sabbath dawned in a typical clear sunny way. The time for Azach's participation in the Sabbath worship slowly drew near. Preparations were complete and the faithful were gathering with their requisite hurried steps that bespoke the joy of hearing God's words.

Approaching the House of Prayer, Joachim told his guest, "We do not have an orchestra for you, but I have had many volunteers cleaning the assembly hall and preparing flowers set out in large vases, and many other things. I hope you enjoy it."

"You flatter me, Joachim," he said. "And I love it," he whispered strongly. They both laughed heartily at this spiritually risqué moment, each aware that they could not carry their joking inside. In their hearts, these spiritual brothers recognized that this humor was rooted in their own resolve to work against their natural instincts, to do everything for the Lord, and to minimize their own recognition. Each of them led the other to serve and to serve well, out of a sense of gratefulness and worship for the Great God they loved.

The hour for the worship to begin arrived. Mary and Hannah were seated in the women's gallery. The reading of the Prophets was finished and the scroll returned to its place. Azach, with properly slow steps, approached the pulpit to deliver his sermon, humbly proceeding without an interpreter. He spoke with clear, measured words as follows.

My dear friends of Nazareth: It is such a pleasure—and an honor—to be asked by the elders of your House of Prayer to present the sermon at this Sabbath worship. I have recently been to Jerusalem to study the twenty-four books of the Scriptures with respect to a very particular point of view. I am very excited share what I have learned with you.

Ours is a very special role on this earth. The God of the universe, the only true god, created us and gave us a lovely world to live in. So many of our ancestors loved it and loved our creator in return for his gifts. Many others have failed to appreciate it, and allowed themselves to be tempted to wander. Many times God allowed them, our forebears, to wander away from Him, but He never forsook them. When they—we—had wandered away, He sought us out and gave us the Law to guide us back to Him. He has been deeply involved with us for well over 3,000 years.

I believe that God wants a genuine relationship with His people. I believe that this means not only Israel as a whole, but each one of us individually. After all, a nation exists only by virtue of the individual people who make it up. This viewpoint, while we see it as valid, we nonetheless often overlook.

To have a relationship with Him, we have a number of things we must do. One of these is to understand Him as much as possible. We must study the scriptures because, in them, we can see His hand and, more importantly, His heart.

In the scriptures, we see that Adam was the first person created by Him. What a blessing was given to Adam. Still, he was a man and not a god, and the spirit of evil was able to gain the upper hand over his destiny. Adam was thus the first to drift away from our Father, the first to gamble away his birthright by arrogantly testing and rewriting what he knew the Father had told him. In Noah, we see a man stunned by God's call to him. Despite being six hundred years old at the time, Noah showed no doubt of the task and set directly to the work, as God instructed him. Through Noah, God gave us all the chance to start again on the path of being His children and enjoying His blessings. Noah had a special relationship with God to carry out a momentous mission for the benefit of all mankind.

In the scriptures, we see that God offered Abraham a special covenant relationship. God gave him a new name and a new life. In extreme advanced age, Abraham was not without his doubts. Even so, God made Abraham, through his wife Sarah, the father of a nation. God tested him and found him to be faithful beyond expectations, and God rewarded him. Abraham shows us all that God seeks a relationship with us so that, through us, God can act for the benefit of us all.

In the scriptures we see Joseph, a man who suffered injustice at the hands of his own brothers, yet remained faithful. He was sold into slavery, yet remained true to his own possibilities. He was surrounded by alien beliefs and remained faithful to God, and God remained faithful to him. Joseph has a special relationship with God and, through him, God blessed a nation of people.

We see Moses, who was orphaned from the earliest of his days. Egyptian law required him to be thrown into the river as a newborn male child of Israel. But God watched over him even then. Raised in the court of Pharaoh, he was very much a son of Adam. He murdered, and ran and hid from Pharaoh. Yet, God worked through him, and though frail and fearful, God emboldened him. This great human leader made himself the servant of the will of

God. God then acted through him to give mankind the greatest of gifts, the law by which our fallen nature could be governed. Moses had to engage in intense encounters with power, but God protected him and, through those moments, spoke to all mankind. It was only Moses' humble service to God's will that allowed him to reflect the grandeur of God. This was a relationship of God and man. This is what God wants—for each of us.

We see that David was another unlikely hero. God used David's youth to highlight His own glory. With Goliath, God worked a wonder through David. In the snares of Saul's jealousy, God's hand was on David. In David's wanderings as an outlaw, God's hand was on him.

From the atrocities born of Saul's jealous frenzy, God protected David. God had a plan for David. David listened to God and fulfilled that plan, despite his failings along the way. They had a relationship and, through that relationship, God blessed His people.

The scriptures are full of God's relationships with His people. We study them and see the potential of God in our midst through our relationships with Him, both as individuals and as a people of God.

But there is another thing we can do, and it is just as essential as reading the scriptures. We must pray to our God. In doing this we come to understand both our own nature and God's nature. In this way, we come to understand, ultimately, our relationship with Him. In this, we come to understand our individual calling from God.

Prayer is a somewhat simple activity and yet, like many simple activities, there are many ways to do it wrong. It seems to us when starting to pray that it requires a great deal of time, effort, and concentration. Many who try to adopt the discipline of prayer in their daily lives are discouraged and find themselves drifting away. They find themselves merely thinking about things, not communicating with God. They may find themselves merely repeating words with little or no growth in any sense of a relationship with God. They find themselves trying to make God do things for them by praying very, very hard. They find themselves waiting for extraordinary 'messages' from God, to no avail or, worse yet, their imaginations create a 'message' from God that anyone but they can see is as ungodly as can be. It is my hope that I can help you improve your efforts and avoid the mistakes of this delightful, essential activity.

Prayer is defined by the reasons to pray, which are rooted in the nature of God and the nature of people as His creatures. The reasons to pray I see as four in number. Primary among these is to worship, to acknowledge God as the God of all beings, of the sun, the moon, the stars, the earth and all of its creatures. The creation of the universe we see in Genesis. We see the immensity of the heavens, the mystery of the sun and the moon, the amazing variety of the creatures of the earth. No one among us could make even one of these things, not one flower, not one goat, not one mountain, not one cloud or rainstorm. He made them all, and continues to make them anew every day. It is obvious, if we attend to it, that God deserves our acknowledgement as God. It is the natural, proper result of the fact that He made us.

The second reason to pray is to thank Him for all He has done. He has no duty to give us anything, yet our lives are full of potential, of the amazing capability we have been born with, and of many things we have made or acquired through those abilities. We look at this beautiful building, made by hands to honor our God. What beauty there is in its design, in its décor, in its adaptation to its glorious purpose. Who did these things? Ancient forebears did these things at great sacrifice of time and energy. They planned, reviewed, thought, worked, and scratched their heads over various crises in the process. However, they persisted and carried it through to the end. These great beams, these great columns, were put into place by human hands inspired by their relationship with God. The paint of the frescoes was applied not only down here where we can easily see, but also at the highest portion of the ceiling. Has any ox done this? Has any bird or dog or fish been able to organize and carry out such a design? No! It is people who are most unique among God's creatures. It is a blessing beyond measure He has given to us. He deserves our constant thanks.

The third element of a prayer is to ask our loving God for the things we need. Wow! After this great catalogue of blessings, which I have just listed, what could we possibly need? We need everything— and nothing! We need goodness—and no evil thing. We need to understand our God, and to let Him lead. Mixed in among all of the blessings He has given us is our human weakness, which we inherit from our first forebear, Adam. The story of Job and his advisors shows how difficult life can be and how difficult it can be to understand God. We have been given the Law and the Prophets for our guidance, and still we drift away. We get bored with God. He confuses us if we do not constantly work to understand Him. He always is in control, and we are not, and that frustrates the part of our nature that is bent on the delusion of control. He gives us what we need not to satisfy our own cravings but to perform our duties to Him, our role as assigned by Him. There is no way to find this role and its details without praying daily and constantly.

The fourth reason to pray is to ask for forgiveness for our wanderings. How do we drift away from God? As I said earlier, Israel as a nation drifted from God many times in its history. I also said that it is only possible for a nation to act through all of its individuals. If every individual were godly and holy, then the nation could not drift from God. The problem may be national, large, and seemingly inexorable, like an enemy army advancing upon us. But the solution is individual. The solution is you. Every one of us, as individuals, has a relationship with God, and a job from God. We are as imperfect as Cain, and must regain the perfection that God designed into us. He will rebuild us according to the Law and the Prophets if we attend to their words in our minds, and to His whisperings in our hearts."

Azach paused and looked around at the congregation, making eye contact with many separate people. Then he spoke in a dramatic whisper.

Well, there it is. Simple, no? Acknowledge God as God; thank Him for the things we have; ask Him for the things we need, and ask forgiveness for our sins. Do this in some way all day, every day, but do not fall into any spiritual errors.

Suddenly louder, he went on. "No!" he shouted dramatically. "Not simple!"

He paused. Then he resumed in a softer, yet dramatic, tone.

As I mentioned earlier, it is a very difficult thing to maintain the practice of prayer. So, I give you one last insight that should make it easier. I mentioned the Law and the Prophets. I mentioned study as well as prayer. In study we come to knowledge. In prayer we come to wisdom and to the integration of all of our scattered pieces of knowledge. I like to say that wisdom is knowledge about knowledge, the truth about the truth. By that I mean that there are many people who know a great many things, but the wise man has related the things he knows to each other and, most of all, to God. Because the man has integrated and interrelated the things he knows, including his own life inside his head, we call him a man of integrity.

So, start with the simple truths. If it is law, you value, start with the Ten Commandments that God gave us through our Father, Moses. Or use a few of your favorite psalms or proverbs. The point is not to overload yourself to the point of distraction, but to go at your own pace. At the same time, do not neglect this joyful time with God. As I said, He has a job for each one of us. It may be as simple as being one of the bricks behind the plaster, or one of the lovely colors in the frescoes painted on it. It may seem to be a position of service or a position of leadership, which is, in fact, just a different kind of a position of service. It may be anything. Moreover, whatever it is today, it may be very different for you tomorrow. But every day God has work for you.

Whatever it may be and however it may change, if it is your pure gift to God, if it is aligned with the Law and the Prophets, if it is wise, and if it is refined daily in the humble discipline of prayer, it will strengthen you as an individual holy person. In that way, your work will bring the people of Israel into the blessings of God; your work will make its families, its cities, and the nation a joy forever.

Azach ended with a dramatic flourish of his right arm upward. He slowly brought it down and then made his way from the pulpit to his place among the leaders.

Azach looked over the congregation. They sat, apparently deep in thought, for a long time. Here and there, people adjusted their seating, but seemed to flow on in thought, like a river in the afternoon, ever moving but at the same time appearing not to change. Azach wondered how his presentation had been received, and worried that he may have been too unconventional in his thoughts. He certainly did not want to create a stir in Joachim's congregation and then move off to his home to leave Joachim to deal with it.

The minister of the ceremony slowly rose to perform the closing ritual and dismiss the congregation. At the end, the congregation moved to the aisle and hallways and began to comment on the sermon they had just heard.

"There is so much there," said one.

"I've never heard a sermon like that," said another. "I've got to think about that one," said a third. "It was like a great spiritual meal; it will feed us for many days to come." "What did you think of that, Mary?" asked Hannah. "I like him. I am going to try to pray that way every day," Mary answered.

THE MEETING

The passing days routinely measured out the recurring seasons and the new milestones in Mary's life. Her womanhood blossomed in her and the other girls in the village in the way it had in countless generations before her. Her skin glowed with color and was as smooth as a fine statue. Her eyes were dark and had a lively sparkle to them. Her hair was mildly curly and dark, peeking around the edge of her scarf. Girl and woman danced in her personality; she was at home with children or adults, leading the young and fascinating the elders. She was old enough to go without her mother, but with a group of her peers, on the familiar path to the well and the market to get the daily water and foodstuffs. She was old enough to put betrothal and marriage on her parents' minds.

One of Joachim's acquaintances was the carpenter, Aaron, who was doing excellent work in the House of Prayer on repairs and new furniture that the elders had ordered. Joachim had met the carpenter's son in the course of the work and liked him. Joachim had heard others talk well of him also. He was ruddy and taught like a hard-working youth so often is and reminded Joachim of his own youth, now hidden behind a modest, mature spread.

"That boy of yours is an excellent worker, Aaron," Joachim said. "Ah, thank you, Joachim. I keep him busy and hope he will walk in the Lord as I have tried to do."

"I hear he is doing well on all accounts," said Joachim. "I see his work here, and I see his attendance at the House of Prayer. He will be a good man."

"We hope and pray so," said Aaron.

Aaron was non-committal at this point but he certainly picked up on the cues Joachim was offering. He knew of Joachim's family and his daughter. From what he had seen of Joachim, it seemed to him to be an idea worth considering. He tucked this moment away to think and pray about. It was no light matter to discuss betrothal, and he wanted to be sure it was properly done in his son's case. He was aware of how crucial this was to his son's future.

When Aaron arrived home, he spoke to his wife, Shoshana. "Joachim is most impressed with our son," he said raising his eyebrows.

"Oh?" she said, understanding completely. "I have spoken to Hannah a number of times in the village and she is always very enjoyable to talk to," she said. "Her daughter Mary is always polite and helpful. She is a quiet thing, but very nice. I have never been disturbed by any of our encounters, and no one else has any bad things to say about them. Perhaps this is something to keep in mind," she said.

After some days, Aaron took Joseph aside and said to him "The time is coming for you to consider a wife. I have had some preliminary conversation with Joachim. You are aware of Mary are you not?"

This news exploded in Joseph's consciousness with vast array of feelings, from fear to impatience to fulfillment and many feelings he had not ever known. From the time he first understood the betrothal process, he had hoped and prayed that his marriage arrangement would be a blessed and God-filled one. His culture demanded that he control his response.

"Yes, I have heard of her and have seen her in the village. She seems to be worthy," he said, delivering the words he had long ago prepared in his mind for this day.

Weeks went by. Joseph worked with his father on the House of Prayer job. Aaron and Joachim had occasional conversations in the course of their respective daily duties and were getting to know each other better.

One evening, Aaron said to his wife, Shoshana, "I think I shall meet with Joachim soon to discuss our children."

"Very well," said Shoshana. Her businesslike response was in sharp contrast to the storm of emotions inside her. Aaron had known her long enough to know this, and he smiled knowingly as he looked in her eyes. She tried to stifle a smile and they shared an embrace that was filled with an awareness of each other and of their faith. Their love had always been grounded in their faith, and they never felt that their household was just the two of them; they felt a partnership with God and that they were always three.

The next day, Aaron saw Joachim at the worksite and sought to catch his eye. However, Joachim was striding earnestly, and the moment did not bear fruit. Likewise, Aaron was not at a point where he could stop his work. He would have to wait for a better moment, perhaps at midday when they would stop for the meal.

Joachim strode to his meeting with Rabbi Jacob to discuss the coming Sabbath preparations. There was to be a special address to the community by the rabbi, and the evening needed to run smoothly. The meeting plodded through the details but eventually was at a point where the staff could break for midday. Joachim began his walk home for the midday meal at a much more relaxed pace. He planned to visit the workers and see how the repairs were coming.

As he approached, he and Aaron greeted each other, and Aaron saw that his moment was at hand. He stepped down from the scaffolding to greet Joachim more personally.

"Ah, Joachim," he said. "How is your day going?"

"Quite well, thank you, Aaron," said Joachim. "Plans for the rabbi's address are coming together."

"It is good when plans come together," Aaron replied. "By the way, I have a matter to discuss with you," Aaron said, quite quietly.

Joachim was already anticipating the nature of this discussion as he said, "I am at your service."

"Well," he said. "I would like you to join me soon to discuss a matter of, shall we say, mutual importance."

"I would be happy to meet with you. Do you have a day in mind?" said Joachim.

"Well," said Aaron, "What evening do you have free?"

"I think it will have to be next week," Joachim said, considering all of the plans he had to arrange for the coming Sabbath. At the same time, he did not want to appear too eager. "What do you think of the beginning of the Third Day?"

"Ah," said Aaron, "that will not do," the little chess game went on. "What about the next evening?"

"I think that will be available," said Joachim.

"Very good," said Aaron. "I will expect you after the dinner hour, if that is convenient for you."

"That will be fine," said Joachim.

Joachim now walked a bit more energetically to his home for the midday meal. A million thoughts played in his mind. Upon arriving home, he greeted Hannah and Mary, remembering the many times Mary had toddled out to greet him as a child. Now she was an able and pretty young woman. Her greeting seemed both mature and warm as she looked up to him and said, "Hello, father," with a welcoming smile.

The modest meal of flatbread, berry spread, and oranges, along with some of the day's water from the well, was prepared today as it had been for countless days over the years. Joachim sat down at their recently acquired inside table, and Hannah and Mary joined him. He looked at Hannah, and she perceived he had something on his mind.

"What does your look mean?" she said.

"I have received an invitation," he said. "A very ....interesting invitation."

Hannah and Mary, each in their own way, tumbled over the possibilities. Hannah said: "And what is this invitation?"

"Aaron, the carpenter working on the House of Prayer, has invited me to his home to discuss 'something of mutual importance,'" Joachim said. "I told him I would be delighted to come."

Nothing more needed to be said. Everyone silently pondered the weight of such an invitation. Mary knew of Joseph, the son of Aaron and Shoshana, and immediately guessed what the conversation at such a meeting might entail. She immediately turned her mind to prayer, quoting the Psalm: "How wonderful are your works, oh Lord."

THE BETROTHAL

Joachim arrived at the carpenter's home. Instead of the customary curtain at the entrance, there was a wonderfully carved entrance door. It had a pair of open panels framed into it with linen curtains mounted on the inside. Overall, it was an effective display of the ability of this carpenter. It was in some contrast to the modesty of the rest of the house, but the home was overall comfortable and well kept.

Joachim called out to announce his presence and was greeted by voices from inside. Shoshana opened the door and offered him a polite greeting.

"Joachim, how nice it is to see you," she said.

Aaron rose and came to the door as well, offering his hand to Joachim, and saying "Welcome, Joachim. We are honored to have you in our home. Please come in."

He entered and offered flowers to Shoshana, saying, "These are for your table."

Shoshana replied, "How sweet of you. Are these from your garden?"

"Yes," Joachim replied. "Hannah gathered them this afternoon."

"Well, she must show me how she grows such lovely flowers," Shoshana said with a little too much self-effacement. She quickly put them into a beautifully turned wood vase and set them on the table, moving her own arrangement to a less obvious place in the home. She also assumed an air of deference to the men and their meeting.

The evening grew in comfort. The two men discussed many things, but somehow the discussion revolved around their memories of their children's growing years. Humorous, poignant, sweet, and sad memories were traded, like small word-gifts. Each of the men took these moments in, evaluated them for puffery, and tucked them away for future consideration. They were each preliminarily comfortable with what they saw and heard. There had been no sense of undue exaggeration, factoring in, of course, normal parental pride.

Aaron finally proposed the terms of a possible betrothal between his son Joseph and Joachim's daughter Mary. "We are similarly blessed, Joachim," he said. "I suggest that Joseph and Mary become betrothed." He offered an appropriate traditional sum of money, and Joachim explained the dowry that he and Hannah had accumulated for Mary consisting of linens and other household furnishings. All in all, it was a reasonable exchange. Joachim said, "I am pleased with the prospects of this betrothal. I am sure God will bless it more than we know."

"May it be so," said Aaron.

Their discussion moved on through some pleasantries until finally Joachim said, "Well, Aaron, I know you have a busy day tomorrow, and I do as well. I will leave you to the rest of your evening."

Aaron responded, "Joachim, I thank you for this productive evening and look forward to a long a special relationship for our two households. Thank you for coming. Please take our blessings to Hannah."

Joachim said, "I will indeed. Thank you, and good night. Good night, Shoshana."

"Good night, Joachim," she said.

Joachim was shown to the beautifully carved door and began his thoughtful walk home. Images tumbled in his head: images of his own betrothal and his own growth as a man in this community and in his own household, as a husband and, in his later years, as a father. There were images of Mary as a sweet toddling infant, as a bright curious child, as a vibrant and wise young girl, and now as a young woman in the full radiance of young adulthood. She was ready to assume her place in the community. It was at once a long-awaited moment and a fresh surprise to him. "How wonderful are your gifts, oh Lord," he prayed in his heart as he walked.

In Aaron's home, a similar kaleidoscope of memories appeared in the parents' minds. They saw their curly-haired, ruddy baby boy picking up everything he came across and saying "Whatsis?" in the angelic voice of a child. They saw him with a bruised and teary face, the first lesson in the potential of even young hearts for violence and domination. They saw him at his passage into manhood and his growing love and understanding of the ancient scriptures. Now, they anticipated his marriage and his taking his full place among the men of the community. It was a transition, but it would be a truly joyous one. They fully expected that their son would be near them, and their grandchildren would take the places that they had carved out and saved for them in their hearts for the past many years.

As Joachim left, Joseph and his mother came into the front room of the house. Joseph needed no further information. By virtue of his knowledge of himself and of life as he had learned it from his parents, from his faith and from his peers, he had sorted things out quite well by now. He had seen other families where the husband treated his wife like the family goat or cow, seldom speaking to her, caring not a bit for her opinion or counsel. He would be better. He would be a good father and provider. He would be fair and care-taking of his wife and respect her for her place as his Eve, his helpmate.

Joachim arrived at his home. It was near the hour to go to sleep but, not surprisingly, Hannah and Mary were awake and waiting for him. They looked at him like cats would, attentive but not staring, waiting for what would be next. He looked at them with reserved contentment and said, "It is arranged."

Hannah looked at Mary and Mary looked at the floor, nearly overwhelmed by the realization. What had been the stuff of many different dreams and musings was now set in stone, immutable. Her future, whatever it would be, was now determined. It was at once a joy and a terror, with every thought about life changing from how it used to be experienced to a new different feeling, one after another, like dough changed to bread on the oven. Her thoughts turned to God and she said, out of faith mixed with a large dose of hope, "How wonderful are your gifts, oh Lord."

THE HUSBAND

Joseph considered his knowledge of manhood and husbanding. He felt good about the days to come. He had no doubts about his ability to make a living as a carpenter, although it most likely would be only modestly comfortable. It was common knowledge in the community how to build a clay brick house. It was a matter of community action when a young man needed to create one for his betrothed. Joseph planned to work on his in his evening hours and to provide for himself and his betrothed through his daily work. His family and friends would occasionally come by the worksite and pitch in, molding the clay bricks and setting them out to bake in the next day's sun, setting the dry bricks in place and slowly forming up the walls of the home. Weeks went by in this way, and the building took shape quite well for a standard two-room home. Nourished by the life of the community, it seemed to grow out of the earth.

Mary looked around at her own home now with a different mindset. She observed the walls, the floors, the windows, and the cooking oven off the back of the house, and felt a new sense of relationship, a new identity, with these things. They were no longer the things of her parents that she worked with in her daily chores. She saw in them now her own future. These were now the tools with which she would work out her own destiny as a wife and mother.

Hannah remembered her own transition time, and an idea occurred to her. She thought of a way to leave Mary alone in the home to "do some thinking."

"Mary," she called.

"Yes, Mother," Mary answered.

"I am going to the market with Joanna, from next door. I won't be long."

"Very well, Mother," Mary answered.

Mary busied herself with the work of the house. There was the evening meal to prepare, and she worked at the arrangement of the oil, olives, and other vegetables that could be cut at this time and not age much in the time from late afternoon until dinner would be served. As she worked, she heard a faint voice call to her.

"Hello, Mary," it said.

She blinked and reviewed her own thoughts, wondering what would make her think that she had heard such a thing.

"Mary. Hello, Mary," she heard again. In an instant, a bolt of fear shot from her neck to her stomach to her legs, and she yelped and started and reeled around, her eyes wide and her hands grasping the edge of the table. She heard from the vision the following words.

Do not be afraid, Mary. Please do not be afraid. I come to tell you that you have found favor with God and are a very blessed woman. God has been with you from the time you were conceived. And now, Listen! You yourself are to conceive and bear a son. You must name him Jesus. He is going to be great and will be called the Son of the Most High. The Lord God will give him the throne of his ancestor David and he shall rule over the House of Jacob forever and his kingdom shall have no end.

Mary stood staring at the vision, her mouth agape. She thought about what she had just heard. The barest beginnings of realizations began to form in her mind.

"I have not known a man," she said, "and—" She could think of nothing further to say at the moment.

She heard the vision say to her, "The Holy Spirit will come upon you, and the power of the Most High will cover you with its shadow. Thus, the child will be holy and will be called the Son of God."

She thought more of this idea and of its impossibility. Then she heard more words from the vision.

"There is something else you should know. Your cousin, Elizabeth, has conceived and will bear a son also. Everyone thought she was barren, but she is now in her sixth month. Know that nothing is impossible with God."

Mary thought of all she had heard. She thought of her parents and their devotion to God. She had always been taught that God leads and we follow, God is our caretaker and we are as servants in His Kingdom. She said to the vision, "I am a servant of God, His handmaid. Whatever He wants of me, I will do. If this is His will for me, let it be."

The vision was no longer. Mary stared at the place it had been. Her mind was swimming. Vague thoughts tumbled in her head and her body quaked. Despite the weather, she felt cold. She did not know whether she was still in her parents' home or halfway in another world, whether she was dying or living. Gradually, she became aware again of the warmth of the day, the sounds of the neighborhood and the smells of the kitchen. She knew that the vision was over now, and tried to remember what she had heard. "What on earth will come of this," she wondered.

Within moments, Hannah arrived back from the market with a fresh cantaloupe. She went into the kitchen and said: "Hello, Mary."

Her greeting was strangely reminiscent of the voice from the vision, and Mary looked up at her mother with a serious concentrating look. "Well, what does this look mean?" Hannah asked.

After a slightly unusual length of time, Mary said, "I need to talk to you, Mother, but I need to do some thinking first."

Hannah looked at her, sensing the new behavior of her daughter. She said in a slow, questioning way, "Very well. Whenever you are ready, I am here for you."

"Let's finish preparing dinner for now," Mary said.

"Very well," said Hannah, resolving in her motherly wisdom not to push on this odd situation. The two worked in their usual way, as they had for the past many years, side by side, without needing to speak or hear instructions. Mary reviewed her thoughts again and again. Images of a baby appeared, surrounded with all of the emotions that her upbringing and her own heart attached to that joyful event. But inevitably her mind turned to the village and the strictures of the faith. People don't have babies this way. It finally dawned on her that she would be accused of conceiving a child with someone other than Joseph. Then her mind suddenly realized the crucial dimension of this problem. Joseph! What will he say? What will he do?

Until now, she had assumed that her mother and father would take her words at face value. Now, she began to wonder what they would make of her story. Would they believe her? She had no idea how she should handle this "blessing" except that she was the handmaid of God as she knew Him, and would pray and trust Him.

Hannah's mind was not still, either. She reviewed all of the possible matters of concern for a betrothed young woman. There was fear of how her man would treat her, fear of sexual activity, fear of childbearing, fear of a million unknowns. Hannah and Mary and all of the women of the village knew of the risks of pregnancy. There were few medical options if the baby would not come out. There was no detailed medical knowledge of bladder and rectum troubles some women suffered, but there was the knowledge of the personal and social problems brought on by the smell of the resulting incontinence of those struck by such birth injuries.

Hannah knew of a very few young women who had become pregnant during betrothal. Since that was legitimate, she was resolved to adapt to that if it were the case. But she knew Mary. That simply could not be it. She speculated that Mary must just be worried about the unknowns and resolved to give her time to think. Patience was the order of the day for now.

Mary did not tell her story to her mother that day. Many days went by. Hannah prayed and waited. Mary prayed and thought. She wondered if the vision were real and whether the message had any meaning to her. She realized that she would know if her menstruation did not come in her next cycle. That would be the truest sign she would have. Then she would take her situation to her parents for their guidance.

COMMUNITY

During this interior time for Mary, Hannah told her one day, "Mary, we need to go to Zippori for new spices and some fabric that we cannot get here in Nazareth. I plan for us to go with Rebecca and two of her friends tomorrow in the morning."

"It's so different from Nazareth," said Mary. "I remember the first time I was here. It was so much bigger and busier. Everything is so strange. I was pretty scared then. I'm glad we have been there before." In the morning they began their walk in the glow of the morning sun. Hannah, Rebecca, Mary and the other women approached the city; its hubbub grew as they walked.

Mary said, "Look at all these people. In Nazareth, we try to speak to everyone we see. Here, it would be impossible to know everyone who is here, and to speak to each of them."

"You would never get anything done," said Rebecca with a laugh.

Even if one's shopping list were short, no trip to Zippori was complete without visiting the many booths at the markets and shops along the streets. This they did with a keen eye for things they might not yet have thought about needing. In Zippori, Marketplace business occurred in many areas of the city, not like the one market in Nazareth. Those that knew Zippori well spoke of the different specialties of the various markets: one excelling in spices, one in various fish from the nearby Sea of Galilee, one having wonderful flowers, one providing breads and wonderful pastries, one having excellent leather goods and fabrics.

As they walked from shop to shop, they suddenly became aware of unusual, most unpleasant sounds. A crowd moved through the street towards a public plaza. The visitors were frozen by the scene. A struggling young woman was being dragged there by some men, authorities of some kind.

"What's happening, Mama," said Mary. Before Hannah could frame any answer, the scene played out. The leaders of the event tied the woman to a post in the plaza, and gathered up their stones. The first stone flew and missed, but the stark reality of the situation was driven home by it nonetheless. The woman devolved into desperate sobbing, unable to make any intelligible sound anymore.

Soon the air was filled with large stones, many so big that the men had to use two hands to throw them. Many hit their mark, their quiet, muffled sounds belying the profound pain they must have created in her poor body, or the cosmically loud sounds they must have created for her when they hit her head. With so many hits happening so quickly, she could barely react to one stone before another one struck her. With each hit, her crying slowly faded, her body sagged more and more and her life ebbed away. Soon her body was lifeless, crouched upon her knees, torso dangling by her arms from the post, her head hanging extremely over her shoulder, now impervious to the stones. Eventually, it became obviously pointless and bad taste to throw any more stones. The crowd of executioners began to disperse, gradually revealing who in the crowd were her family and friends who would release her and take her to her rest.

Hannah looked at her daughter and saw in her face the chill that had settled in her soul. Mary had heard of the law and had word-knowledge of what she had just seen. Now, the sights and sounds of it were seared into her being. Her mind struggled to see the justice in it.

"The woman was screaming for mercy! For all of its riches, mercy is in short supply in Zippori today," said Mary.

Despite the conflict in her own heart, out of social and religious training, Hannah said, "It is a very bad thing that she must have done. It is sad for her and her family."

"I know the law," snapped Mary to her mother. "But she was just a young woman. She was no criminal. She did not deserve this!" Mary's voice had steadily increased in intensity and she displayed an assertiveness and anger that her mother had never seen before. She immediately thought of Mary's odd behavior in Nazareth, and put the two together. It hit her like lightning that Mary was possibly with child. She stared at Mary. Mary looked at her Mother and instantly looked away.

"We should find the things we came for and get back to Nazareth," said Mary, tersely.

"Yes, we should," said Rebecca, peacemaking. As they went off in search of their spices and fabric, it seemed like a different day, a different place, a different life that they were living. They returned to Nazareth with these images relentlessly fixed and replaying their minds. Each of them knew that it was not impossible to see herself in such a circumstance if she were accused of such an offense. They knew that it would be a long time before this day would allow their own natural life-rhythm to return.

When Hannah and Mary returned to their house, Hannah said, "I think it's time we talked, Mary."

Mary looked at her a long time.

"I know your cycle is late." Hannah said, with an unusual intensity. Mary knew her mother would have been thinking and observing. Slowly, Mary joined her hands under her chin and explained.

"Very well, mother. The day you went to the market with Joanna, I had an experience, actually a vision. It was a glorious being, like a person, but very much not like a person. It must have been an angel. It spoke to me. It told me that I would have a son, that he would be conceived in me by the Holy Spirit, and told me many other things." Mary's calmness gradually failed her as she saw the concern in her mother's face. Mary stopped to allow her mother to process what she had been hearing.

"So, you are with child," Hannah said.

"I believe so," said Mary.

"Have you had relations with Joseph?" asked Hannah, her voice rising.

"I have not had relations with anyone," said Mary, defensively. Hannah paused. "That is not believable," she said, totally perplexed.

"The angel said that all things are possible with God," Mary said. As the two women looked at each other, the intimacy of their years together provided them a trust that prevented panic from controlling them. However, the wonderful images that flowered in Hannah's mind when the betrothal was announced were now dying flowers. What would the community do with this knowledge? What would be the necessary actions to take care of this situation, actions that would be, to a great extent, beyond their control as women in their society? The images of the terrible day in Zippori, when they witnessed a stoning, they realized, could be lived out again here.

There was also the impact on Joachim's status in the community. There could be harsh consequences for him as well.

"Mary," Hannah said. "This is not believable. I know you. I cannot believe that you would have relations with anyone other than Joseph, or that you would have relations apart from God's expectations, or that you would make up a lie to cover it up. Honestly, daughter, I simply do not know what to believe. I need to hear this again. Tell me this again."

Mary started again, at the beginning, sensing now her mother's faith in her. She went into greater detail and presented her experience as best she could. This time, Mary was also able to mention that Elizabeth was also with child, as the angel had told her. When she had finished, Hannah said, "Well, this is truly an amazing message.

Hannah and Mary were silent a long time. Finally, Hannah said, "We will pray and trust the Lord. If Elizabeth is with child, that will be a great confirmation of the message. We will wait to see if that is so."

They thought together in a communal silence, standing there in the kitchen, each with their arms folded. Hannah finally moved toward Mary and embraced her daughter.

"How wonderful are your gifts, oh Lord," she said. After a few moments, they ended their embrace and Hannah said, "We will have to discuss this with Joachim."

Mary looked in her mother's eyes with a daughter's trust and nodded approvingly.

Some hours later, the devoted husband and father Joachim came home from his day of attending to the House of Prayer. His mind was filled with the progress of the work on the refurbishing and the other administrative details he had to manage. He came in the front doorway, moved the curtain aside, and greeted his two ladies.

"Good evening, Father," said Mary.

"Good evening, husband," said Hannah, with a wry smile.

This was the first clue to Joachim that he had better transition to his home life from his business life. The ladies were well aware that he needed his time to transition and made it a practice to leave him to his thoughts for a while when he arrived home. They went about the final preparations for the evening meal and, when it was ready, announced it to him.

"Ah, thank you, my dear ladies," he said, as he often did. "You treat me like a king. It is such a joy to come home to you both."

At this, their anxiety rose a bit, and they looked knowingly at each other. Joachim said the blessing and they began the meal. As it progressed, the moment arrived where it seemed opportune to tell him their news.

"Joachim," said Hannah, "we have something important to tell you. Actually, Mary needs to tell you."

Joachim looked wonderingly at Hannah, and then somewhat officially at Mary, and authorized her to proceed. She told him the details of her experience. This unbelievable story and its very logical motivation, in most circumstances, crashed into his thoughts. He sensed the fragile nature of his life in the House of Prayer, and the risk to it posed by this news. He sensed the risk to his family, to the wedding plans, to his relationship with Aaron, and with every other man in the village. In sum, this woman, this daughter, posed a threat to nearly everything he had built up in his life. His conflict was visible in his face and his tone.

"This is not believable," he said.

"I put my faith in the Lord, as you have taught me, and I pray daily for His protection," said Mary. "It is the truth, Father."

He was silent a moment. Finally, he said, "And you, Hannah?"

"I know Mary, and I know your faith," she said. "The angel said that, with God, all things are possible, and said that Elizabeth is also with child, in her sixth month. I think that it will be a very powerful sign if that is true."

Joachim looked at his ladies. He reflected on everything he knew of them. It was not any more logical to doubt their sincerity than it was to doubt the possibility of this story being true. Faith in God was the only pathway through this problem.

He went to Mary and smoothed his hands on each side of her head and said, "I must believe you, if you tell me it is true. I will put my trust in you, and pray, and take each day as it comes." After some time, Joachim said, "We must speak to Aaron and Joseph." Again, Mary looked into the eyes of a loving parent, and nodded.

Joachim went the next day to the House of Prayer and looked at it with fresh eyes. It was the same; he was the one in new circumstances. He sought out Aaron in the work area and found him up on the scaffolding. Aaron greeted him warmly and climbed down. When he was down, Joachim said to him, "We need to talk about something very important and urgent. Can you come now?"

Aaron thought a bit, and looked at Joachim. Then he looked back at the scaffolding, assessed the work that would proceed over the next few hours and said, "Yes, I can leave the work to the rest of the workers for now. What is it, Joachim?"

"We need privacy. We will go to my home. I will tell you when we get there."

Aaron motioned to Joseph that he was leaving for a while. Aaron knew that they could handle the work while he was gone. Joseph would be left to answer any questions that might arise.

They strode to Joachim's house. Joachim spoke to Aaron and hit him with a question he did not expect. "How strong is your faith, Aaron?" "What could you possibly mean?" said Aaron.

"I am sorry, Aaron. I am not questioning your faith. It is just that what you are about to learn will challenge your faith a great deal and in many ways. It will challenge not only your faith in me and my household, but in God as well."

"What is this all about, Joachim?" said Aaron with some impatience in his tone.

"Please be patient. We will explain all when we get to my home."

"We?" asked Aaron. He was beginning to piece this together. They walked on and soon arrived at Joachim's home. He called out to the women, and they appeared in the doorway of the home.

"Hello, Aaron," said Hannah as warmly as she could without overdoing it. "Please come in."

"Hello, Hannah," said Aaron, his uncertainty apparent.

"I have indicated to Aaron that we have a matter of importance to explain to him, and he has graciously taken time away from his work to come here at my request," said Joachim. "Let us begin. Mary is the best one to explain it. Go ahead, Mary."

Once again, calmed by prayer and her faith, Mary told her improbable story to a person who was not likely to believe it. Aaron processed what he had heard. "You are with child, and you expect us to believe that it was conceived by an angel?" Aaron said.

Mary was hit by the comment and said, "The angel was only the messenger. The Holy Spirit conceived it." Somehow, this comment did not seem any more convincing.

"This is not believable, Joachim," Aaron said. "I know she is your daughter, and I have heard you say that you have great faith in her. But this is not believable."

"I told you that this would challenge your faith in me as well as in God. It is likewise a challenge to my faith. However, I urge you for the time being to pray and trust in the Lord. The angel's message was clear that all things are possible with God."

Aaron said, "I am in a similar position to you, Joachim. I respect you a great deal. We have had an excellent relationship up to now. You ask me to pray and trust the Lord patiently. I will do that, for you. But I am very doubtful, my friend; very doubtful."

"Many times, we do all we can do and must trust the Lord from there. I thank you, Aaron, truly from my heart."

"We must tell Joseph as soon as possible. Will you come to our home this evening?" asked Aaron.

"Certainly," said Joachim. "We will come after the dinner hour."

"Very well. May God be our guide." Aaron looked at Mary, but could not bring himself to smile. "Let us get back to our work," he said, and rose to take his leave.

"I will go back with you, if you will allow me," said Joachim.

"Certainly, Joachim," said Aaron, and the two men walked back to the House of Prayer, saying very little.

92

The evening arrived, Joachim walked to his home, and the evening meal passed quietly. When they were finished, they rose to go to Aaron's home. They walked quietly, understanding ahead of time what would transpire. They would explain to Joseph that he needed to hear what Mary had to say, and they would give the conversation over to her. The now familiar, improbable story would once again be told to someone who would find it very hard to believe. And so it went, once again.

When she was done, Joseph looked in stunned silence at this waif and her story. The silence went on and on. Finally, he said abruptly, "Thank you for coming. I must consider what I am to do." He left the room quickly.

"We will go, Aaron. I am sorry for this trouble. I only ask that you continue to pray and trust."

"I will endeavor to do so," said Aaron, surprised at his own formal tone. It did not seem to anyone that any more words would be helpful.

Joseph's reaction had surprised Mary, and she now felt totally alone. This turn of events crushed her spirit, and she broke down in tears on the way home. Everything she had grown to expect for herself as she became a woman in this village was now threatened. If Joseph rejected her, her life would be totally cut off from all that she knew and was prepared for. She was confused, without a reference point. She had prayed and she had trusted, but it appeared that God had not heard. Hannah walked with her arm around her daughter and tried to console her. "Remember, Mary: Nothing is impossible with God."

"I know I must believe and trust the Lord," Mary said. "It is so hard right now."

"It often is, my dear," said Joachim. "It often is. But if it were easy for us, it would not show His power. To everything there is a season.

This is our waiting season." Back in Aaron's home, Joseph's thoughts no longer were taken up with homebuilding and husbanding. He now thought only of the impossibility of this situation. What could he do now? He would talk to his father and get his advice, but ultimately this was his own matter. He got up and went to his father.

"Father, what is your view of this problem?" he asked.

"It is not believable," he said. "The girl is apparently quite serious about her faith, but other girls have become with child without marriage. It is frequent enough that we have laws about it. My wish for you is that you would have a decent, respectable marriage. That means that you should divorce Mary. I think she and her family are respected enough that she can safely be sent away, perhaps where her cousin lives, and we can have a smooth ending to this problem."

"Thank you for your thoughts, Father," Joseph said. "My thoughts are running in that direction as well. I cannot take her based upon this story that I cannot believe, that no one can believe. I would be considered a total fool all of my life. I will pray and decide soon."

Over the course of the next few days, as he prayerfully reviewed his own faith and his own common sense, he gradually became resolved along his original thoughts to divorce her and send her away where she could safely have her child. That decision, once finally made, put his mind at rest, and he finally felt he could get a good night's sleep. He went again to his father and said, "Father, I have decided to do as we discussed. I shall divorce her and send her away."

"I think it is a just and fair thing to do, Joseph," Aaron said. "I shall talk to Joachim tomorrow."

"Very well," said Joseph.

Joseph then went to his mat. He resolved to think about untangling the other details of this problem another day. For now, his decision made, he just wanted to sleep. Sleep he did.

As he slept, he dreamt. A vision came to him with a feeling of strangeness and familiarity at once.

"Joseph," he heard. "Joseph, son of David. Do not be afraid to take Mary home to be your wife. She has conceived what is in her by the Holy Spirit. She will give birth to a son, and you must name him Jesus, because he will save his people from their sins."

Joseph slept on until morning. When he awoke, he scoured his mind to recall the dream. It was fairly clear in his mind. It was the opposite of what he had planned to do. He and his father were getting ready to go to their work in the House of Prayer, which was nearing completion. He went to his father and said, "Father, things have changed."

"What do you mean, Joseph?" said Aaron.

"Things have changed. I had a very strong dream last night. I heard an unearthly voice tell me not to be afraid to marry this girl and that her son is of God, and all that she has said is true. I believe I should heed this voice and marry her."

Aaron looked at Joseph in disbelief, staring, thinking, unmoving.

"It is not believable," he said, sternly, word by word.

"I know, father," Joseph said. "But her angel said all things are possible with God. And he gave her a sign in her cousin, Elizabeth. And now I have had a message delivered to me. The reasons are building up. In faith, we must follow what we believe God wants. I now believe this," he said.

"It will be challenging," said Aaron.

"I know that it will. I can understand if you distance yourself from this thing, and from Mary and me, but I am convinced now."

Aaron thought a while. Then he said, "I will not abandon you, Joseph. It will not be easy, nor will it be impossible." Then he said, with a wry smile, "It will just be life."

Joseph smiled similarly.

"Well, let us tell your mother, and then go and see Joachim and Hannah," said Aaron. They went to tell Shoshana, and the scene seemed eerily to repeat itself in their household. Finally, Shoshana understood and deferred to her men as her culture had trained her. She did not concern herself greatly with whether she agreed; hers was just to make it work as well as possible, and that she would do.

Though it was morning, they all resolved to walk to Joachim's home to share their decision. Aaron felt that the workers would know enough by now of the project to busy themselves reasonably well until he and Joseph could get to the job. As they walked, their happiness built, despite the social risks this thing posed. As they approached Joachim's house, they were nearly boisterous in their talking.

At the door curtain, Aaron called out "Hellooo, Joachim! Hellooo!"

Joachim was up and dressed, and came to the door full of confusion. "Why, Aaron! Joseph! Shoshana! Hello and good morning to you." As he saw their demeanor, he picked up on it and said with a small smile, but still confused, "Please come in. I hope all is well."

Hannah and Mary also came forward to join the circle.

"Better than you might think, I should say," said Aaron. "Joseph has some news for you," said Aaron, gesturing towards Joseph with his open hands.

Joseph looked at Mary and said, "I was blessed with a vision last night in a dream."

Mary caught her breath and put her hands to her mouth.

"The message," he continued, "was that your child is of the Holy Spirit, and all the rest that the angel told you, and that I should not be afraid to take you as my wife. It goes against all reasonable thinking, but not against faith. So, I am not afraid, and I will take you."

Mary quaked with sobbing, and Hannah reached around her to support her. Joachim looked at the family before him and said, "Again, I thank you for your faith in our household, and I thank God for the faith each one of us has in Him. We in this house are fond of saying 'How wonderful are your gifts, oh Lord.'"

"Amen, and so they are," said Aaron.

As they processed this turn of events, they gradually returned to a sense of normalcy.

"We are now late for our daily work, but we should celebrate this moment. When can we gather for a meal together?" Aaron said.

"Well, soon, I should think," said Joachim. "What about the next Second Day. We will prepare the meal here somewhat earlier than the normal dinner time. It occurs to me that we need to plan a wedding as soon as we can."

"Ah, yes," said Aaron, looking at the two betrothed children. "Very soon."

THE VISIT

Mary looked up through red, teary eyes. "What about Elizabeth? I think I need to go to see Elizabeth," said an unusually assertive Mary. Everyone thought about that, and discussed it. Slowly they came to agreement that the wedding could wait until Elizabeth's child was born.

"But surely you can't go alone," said Hannah. Your father and I are not well enough for such a journey." They pondered this a moment, and Hannah finally said "I will ask your uncle Jonathan to go with you."

Joachim said, "I guess that would be best. I really do not think you or I can make the journey, Hannah. I think we must stay here. If Jonathan goes along, she will be safe."

Joachim then said to Mary "I will see if there is a good caravan organizer we can trust to know the way and provide us some safety for your trip. There is usually news in the square. As soon as there is a group traveling that way that can give you a safe way to travel there, you shall go."

Their plans in agreement, the two families parted. Joseph and his parents made their way towards their home. Joseph and Aaron saw Shoshana home and made their way to the worksite.

Joachim had left them in order to go more directly to the House of Prayer to take up this day's work.

On the way, Joachim asked the local merchants if they knew a good agent to arrange for the travel of his daughter and nephew, Jonathan, to the hill country of Judea. Merchants were in constant motion over the roads and knew the ways from city to city. Joachim knew only of the way to Jerusalem and Zippori and various others of the surrounding communities, but not the way over the seventy miles south to Elizabeth and Zachary's home. He knew that one of the benefits of the Hellenistic Roman yoke was the vastly improved roads and the commerce they brought. It enabled everyone to build stronger ties with people farther away than ever before. News and business deals and goods traveled more quickly now. He was confident that travel would be relatively simple. Walking as part of an organized caravan would afford the safety of numbers and professional defenders as well as men who knew the way.

The merchants in the village all agreed that the best way to find a caravan traveling to anywhere was to travel the four miles to Zippori. This Roman outpost was vastly larger than Nazareth, and there were many caravan organizers and operators there. Joachim asked these Nazareth merchants if they knew of a particular operator they would recommend. They each recommended a few names, but the one that came up most often was Samuel of Zippori.

"I will talk to him, and tell him how highly you recommend him," Joachim told the Nazareth merchants.

Joachim then went to his duties at the House of Prayer. In the course of the day, he made plans with his staff for him to be away the next day. Throughout the workday, he was distracted by the challenge and the excitement of his daughter's journey.

Hannah and Mary went to Jonathan's house, on the far side of the village. He kept some goats and sheep on a small plot of land at the edge of town. He had a couple of sons who were old enough to trust with the care of the animals. That would enable him to be away for some time with Hannah and Mary.

They approached the house and called out their greeting in the musical sing-song of friendly women's voices. "Jonathan! Rivka! Hello!"

Rivka appeared at the doorway with all of the usual cheer and delight of having visitors. "Oh, Hannah and Mary! How are you?! Come in, come in."

They shared hugs and kisses all around and soon turned to discussing various bits of news. Mary and Hannah waited patiently until the discussion came around to Elizabeth. Eventually Rivka spoke up and said "Jonathan, tell them about Elizabeth."

"Oh, yes!" said Jonathan. "We have received a message from Elizabeth that she is expecting a baby of all things! Can you believe it, at her age?

"No!" said Hannah with a windstormy voice of surprise. Mary silently crossed her hands over her mouth in surprise, for her own reasons. "You are kidding!" said Hannah.

"No," said Rivka. "The pregnancy is in the seventh month now. It won't be long!"

Hannah's eyes met Mary's and went back to Jonathan's. "Well, how is she? Is everything all right? How I would love to go and see her," said Hannah.

Even knowing the news already, Mary was still shocked by this confirmation.

"You really look surprised, Mary," said Jonathan.

"Well, I am, Uncle Jonathan. This is very big news. It may be a significant child," said Mary.

After a moment, Hannah spoke up and said, "Is anyone going to see her? I know your boys are able to manage things for a time if you were to go."

"Well, I have considered it, but it is nearly four days of travel," said Jonathan.

Hannah said, "Well, I think it would be good for Mary to go and help her, don't you? I would love to go, too, but I am thinking it would be very expensive for her and me both to go, and I am getting such pains in my knees these days."

Jonathan replied, "I am sure it would be a very welcome thing to her. And, in the larger picture of things, it would be good for Mary to be there, but it is quite a journey."

"Well, with you along it should be good," said Hannah. "Mary won't be any trouble."

"I bet we'd have a good time, despite the traveling," said Jonathan, as the decision came to fruition in his mind. "I guess we'll do it," he said. "Is that alright, Mary?"

"Oh, yes," said Mary. "I've never traveled that far before, but with you along, Uncle Jonathan, I'm sure it will be fine."

They moved on to discuss other things in the way family members do, and eventually the time came for them to return home. The hugged and kissed all around again, and Hannah and Mary set out for home. When they arrived, Joachim was not yet home from his work. The women made the evening meal ready. Joachim arrived soon after the women did, and they filled him in on the news of Jonathan being willing to go with Mary to Elizabeth's house.

"Very good," said Joachim. "There is a caravan leaving for the south in four days. I will check with Jonathan to see if he can join that one or wait for the next."

After the evening meal, Joachim went to visit Jonathan and Rivka. Jonathan felt that he could organize the work of his small farm among Rivka and the boys and that he could be ready to go in four days. Joachim assured him that he would check in on Jonathan's household each day.

"Oh, don't worry about that," Jonathan said. "Our neighbors are good people. They will watch things here."

Joachim said, "Nonetheless, I will visit here often."

Jonathan offered his hand and nodded gratefully to Joachim.

"Very good," said Joachim. "We will have Mary ready as well. The caravan will leave at sunrise on the fourth morning from now. We must travel to Zippori to join it, so we will have to leave quite early to get there in time."

Jonathan thought a bit. He reviewed the idea and finally said, "I have a number of donkeys here. Why don't we use one of them for Mary to ride on for the journey?"

"That would be perfect," said Joachim. "I will certainly pay you for the use of the animal." As Jonathan put up his hands and turned his face to the side, indicating that payment would not be necessary, Joachim continued, "I was planning to rent one from Samuel of Zippori, but it would be better to have one that we all know."

"Absolutely," agreed Jonathan. "But this is family and there is no need to pay anybody."

"Well, Jonathan, I am entirely willing to pay, and you are entirely welcome to payment. I hear that Samuel charges only a couple of sesterces for the journey. I would gladly pay you that."

"Ah, Joachim, I respect you for your offer, but I have long believed we should not make money from family or friends. It will all even out over time."

"Very well, Jonathan. How about, then, if you and Rivka spend the evening before we leave with us so that we can all say proper goodbyes? We will provide a good sendoff meal."

"I am sure that it would mean a great deal to Rivka. We will bring the donkey with us and be ready to go."

"Very good, Jonathan," said Joachim. "An adventure, eh?"

"That it is," said Jonathan.

They said their goodbyes, and Joachim headed to his home.

"It is all arranged," he told his ladies.

"We must tell Joseph," said Mary. "Please, let us go to Joseph's house, Papa."

"We can all go," said Joachim, looking to Hannah for her unspoken opinion. Hannah readied herself for the walk to the carpenter's home.

They arrived in short order and called out. Their greetings were answered, and their hosts were very glad to see them. They shared pleasantries all around, and Shoshana took a special loving interest in her new daughter-in-law. Joseph went to Mary and took her hands in his.

"You children go off and talk," said Aaron.

Mary and Joseph went to the rear yard, and she told him of the plans for the journey.

Joseph said, "My father feels that it would be better if I stay here and finish our house and prepare for our wedding. I disagree, and feel that I should be with you on this journey, but I see the wisdom of his decision. I know your uncle will care for you very well, and for me to be along would only complicate things on the journey and cause us to fall behind in our preparations. We do not have much time to spare, do we?"

Mary wryly shook her head "no."

Joseph paused and looked at his betrothed young woman. "I will miss you very much, and will have you and our special child in my prayers every moment," he said.

Mary returned his look and told him, "There is no better man than you for this child. I will return as soon as I can."

In the front of the house, Joachim said, "We came to tell you that Mary's journey to the hill country to see her cousin is all arranged. She and her uncle will travel with one of the caravans of Samuel of Zippori. It should be as comfortable and safe as any other way to make the journey. Jonathan will provide her one of his donkeys for her to ride, so it should work out well."

Aaron said, "Joseph and I have talked and feel that it would be best if he remains here to work on their house and prepare for the wedding, since there is little time to waste before it. I hope that is agreeable to you."

Joachim said, "Yes, it is a good decision. There are good reasons on both sides of the question, but I do think this is the wiser course of action. However, we should have a meal together the evening before they leave, and, on the morning of the departure, we will make sure there is time for us to stop and say goodbye. Come to our home for the evening meal together. Jonathan and Rivka will be there also."

"Hannah and Shoshana can plan what our household can contribute to the evening," said Aaron, receiving an approving look from his wife.

With the plans all made, the elders called out for the missing betrotheds, said their goodbyes, and made their way home.

Over the next three days, they prepared for Mary to travel to see Elizabeth. The logistics were not terribly difficult. Travelers did not carry much with them. Jonathan would take care of his own money and the money that Joachim gave him to take care of Mary's expenses. Mary was going to take only one change of clothes. Because of the occasionally cold weather that the people experienced in the winters or in the high country, most people had a pair of sturdy shoes in addition to daily sandals. She would use these mostly for the journey and was grateful that they were well broken in. She would also have a good substantial cloak for sleeping. Many nights, she knew, would be spent on the ground. Also, she would have a flask of water that would have to be filled frequently. Food would be provided at the evening inns along the way for a fee, of course.

With their preparations made, the reality settled in on them. It was a time of bitterness and sweetness. There was a risk that injury or disease would befall one of them, or that the caravan would not be able to discourage such marauders as there may be in the hills along the way. Still, the risk of these things was reasonably low. The families looked forward to the news of Elizabeth and to the life lessons that Mary would learn from this chance to be with Elizabeth in her last months of pregnancy. It was another time to trust in the Lord, after taking all the precautions they could themselves.

The afternoon before Mary was to leave, Rivka and Jonathan arrived with their donkey. They tied it to the mulberry tree in the back yard and provided it some fodder on the ground.

Aaron and Shoshana also arrived with Joseph. Inside, the preparations were underway for the great meal, and the aroma of roasting beef filled the home.

"Someone has been to the market!" said Aaron. "It smells wonderful," he said to Hannah.

Wine was poured, food was presented, and the first fledgling bonds of extended family began to grow. Joachim blessed the meal, and Aaron raised a toast to the young betrothed couple. They all shared the food of the table and family stories of the childhoods of Mary and Joseph. The evening wore on and the bonds of relationship grew more vibrant. Eventually, Aaron spoke up.

"Shoshana, Joseph, we should be on our way and let these people get a good night's sleep." Hugs and kisses went around, and the guests departed. Mary and Hannah cleaned up the food and dishes, and finally everyone was ready to retire for the evening.

Morning came on the day of departure. Everyone was up early and the house was abuzz. The money, the cloaks, the changes of clothes, the shoes, and the water were tallied over and over. Soon the time to leave was at hand. Mary, Jonathan and Joachim readied themselves for the walk to Zippori, via Joseph's house.

Soon they heard hellos at the door, and Aaron, Shoshana and Joseph appeared. "We simply could not wait," said Shoshana. "We also felt it would be helpful to come here and save you the trouble of coming by our house.

"Very good, very good," said Hannah. "Welcome. They were just about to leave for your home, but now you are here, and we can all send them on their way."

Joseph and Mary went out away from the crowd of families for their own time together.

"I will miss you very much," said Joseph. "Please be very careful."

"Jonathan will be with me. It will be alright," she said." Besides, God is with us, if we put our faith in Him."

"That is true," said Joseph, "and so we must."

They simply looked at each other, seemingly forever, each taking in the details of the other's face, to remember over the next three months. "Alright, you two," yelled Jonathan "time to go."

Joseph and Mary returned to the crowd of well wishers and did their final round of hugs and goodbyes. Joseph too gave Mary a hug that was a little longer than the rest, one which conveyed to her the comfort and security he would provide her the rest of her days. She would cherish it all during her time away.

Hannah and Rivka hugged the two departing travelers, shed tears of love and promised to keep them in their daily prayers. With a great deal of difficulty, the travelers courageously pulled themselves away and took the first steps of their journey. Joachim was happy that his own time to leave them had not yet come and that there would be a few hours more with his dear daughter.

The way to Zippori was well worn. Someone from Nazareth went there practically every day. The path was smooth and free of challenges, if not straight. The trio made their way to the city and Joachim guided them to where Samuel was gathering his caravan. The chaos and noise was unnerving to Mary. "I'm sure glad you're here, Uncle Jonathan," she said, looking at him with big eyes and a smile that only slightly hid her concern about all these strangers who were now her world.

What Jonathan and Joachim did not say was that there was real difficulty and danger in a trip such as this. The heat at midyear accelerated the drain on the energy of both people and animals.

Night, as well, could be chilly and dangerous. Wild animals to worry about included lions. Occasionally, stories of wild boars circulated, and their ferocity was legendary.

"We'll be fine, Mary," he said. "Most people will just keep to themselves and will be generally nice to each other. We all know we are in this together. If there is any trouble, it will generally be among the people involved and will not affect the rest of us. Samuel will have to deal with them if they are too troublesome. If they can't behave, he will make them travel at the end of the caravan of maybe send them back on their own. There is too much work for each of us to do to allow squabbles to waste our energy and time." Jonathan sounded, at least, as though he knew what he was talking about, and Mary felt better.

Jonathan and Mary found a place to be in the caravan, not too far from the front where the dust and dung would be less than if they were farther back. The front places were all secured by wealthier persons who paid a higher fee for the comfortable privilege.

Eventually, Samuel's men went through the crowd sounding their horn trumpets, indicating that the caravan was about to depart. The nervous energy mounted; people and animals stood and fidgeted. Everyone reviewed their belongings and said their last bits of conversation with their loved ones. Finally, shouts went from the front to the rear of the caravan, and the river of living things began to flow as if floodgates had been opened. Mary gave her father a last tearful hug, and Jonathan gave him a sincere manly embrace. Off they went to take their place, Mary walking at this stage to save the donkey's strength and to use the strength she had built up overnight. She knew that riding all day long was about as undesirable as walking all day long.

The dust was already rising in the orange glow of the sunrise. The fear of the journey slowly gave way to interest in the changing scene. The group developed its own rhythm and settled into a quick but steady movement that most people could handle. If anyone was uncertain of being able to keep up, they probably were not in the crowd in the first place.

Over time, the landscape slowly changed from the familiar to the unfamiliar. The city faded away and new images paraded before them. Pasture areas and other buildings came and went. It was almost entertaining to watch the slow unveiling of worlds Mary had never even dreamed of in her few years of life. Through the dust, dung, and noise Mary said to herself, "How wonderful are your blessings, oh Lord."

Throughout the day, the caravan moved forward, following a winding path southeastward, southwestward, and back. Jonathan said to Mary, "We are going down to the Jordan River because it will be lower and smoother to travel, and the water will be closer."

"Mmmmh," said Mary, seeing the practicality of the idea.

They passed various stone markers, which gave them confidence that Samuel's men knew what they were doing. Every hour or so, Jonathan would tell Mary to take a drink of water from the flask she had brought.

"How far will we go today?" asked Mary.

"Well, dear, there are inns set at about twenty miles apart. That is about as far as is reasonable for a caravan to go each day. When we get to the inn, we will stop for the evening."

"Twenty miles? How long will that take?" asked Mary.

"I expect the sun will still be up some, but it will be evening. We will probably stop to rest briefly in the morning, at noon and in the afternoon. If you imagine how long it took us to walk to Zippori this morning, we have about five times that much to do today. We will be east of the mountains and probably near the river by then."

"So, it will be four days?" asked Mary.

Jonathan nodded his answer.

"How will we find Elizabeth's house?"

Jonathan said "I know the way from a marker on the road just south of the third night's inn. I have asked if there are people going up the road to Ephraim, and hopefully there will be some others with whom to travel that final part of the journey. If not, you and I can do it. We'll be fine."

And so, the day passed. At midday, Jonathan and Mary ate the bread they had brought and were reasonably free of hunger. Mary took the opportunity to ride the donkey during the hottest part of the day. The trudging proceeded, and the sun moved toward the west. Eventually the afternoon break arrived and passed, and the caravan moved forward again. Finally, the "inn" appeared on the horizon, and many people gazed in unbelief at the meager structure.

Slowly, the details of the inn revealed themselves. It seemed to be more of a four-sided pen than an inn. Its primary function was to make sure that wild animals were fenced out and the caravan's animals were secure from predators. In the large walled area, everyone searched for their piece of the turf for the evening. One corner was set aside for the animals, and Jonathan had to take his donkey there and leave it in the custody of the animal guard provided by Samuel's men. In other areas, fires were built by the wealthier people and all shared in them as best as the crowd would allow, mostly by watching them and using the light they afforded. Vendors moved through the crowd touting their various foods and beverages. Mary and Jonathan filled their water flasks at the well and bought a small confection of sautéed meat chips and vegetables, wrapped in a flatbread. In the circumstances, it was as welcome as a feast.

People eventually settled down for the evening, laying on the ground and wrapping up in their cloaks. Again, Samuel's men provided some guard services through the night. Some time before sunrise, the aroma of sautéed meat and vegetables again wafted through the camp. Morning arrived with the same men moving about the camp and shouting for all to arise and be ready to depart when the sun broke over the horizon. Vendors again went through the camp and offered food for sale. People ate, visited the latrines, drank their water, filled their flasks, redeemed their animals, and prepared for departure. The day gave every indication of being hot and sunny, as innumerable days were. And so it was. The people trudged to the morning break, to the midday meal, the afternoon break, and the inn for the evening this day, just like the day before and just like they would tomorrow.

The days wore on. Mary endured the heat and the work of travel by retreating into her mind and tumbling thoughts. She no longer wondered if that baby was really in there. She imagined all of the things she had seen of the process, imagined herself with the great belly that she might have difficulty getting her hands around. She thought of her friends and family who would be there to help, just as she was going to help Elizabeth. She recounted psalms and prayers, reviewed images of the angel and his message. It made the time go by and brought her a deeper relationship with her future.

On the evening of the third day, she began to feel more excited. Tomorrow would end their long trip, and she would see Elizabeth, her mother's niece. "We are getting close, Uncle Jonathan," she said.

"Yes. Tomorrow evening we will have a real house to sleep in and real food to eat and maybe even get to take a bath and wash our clothes. I don't mind telling you that you are getting pretty smelly," he jested.

Mary scrunched her face at him, and they both enjoyed the joke.

They performed their evening disciplines and prepared for sleep. Despite the excitement of the oncoming day, the work of the journey had tired them again, and they slept well until the morning wakers and the aroma of the breakfast foods moved through the crowd. The process was getting to be routine, going smoother each day. As the sun broke over the horizon to their left, the caravan again took on a coordinated action like a huge snake moving down the western shore of the Jordan.

This was the fourth day of the journey, the day they would break away from the main caravan and go with a smaller group moving westward on the Ephraim Road. They proceed on southward with the caravan until the road came into view. As they approached, Samuel's men came back through the crowd yelling for people intending to head west on the Ephraim Road. "Watch for the man with a red flag. Gather on the westward road behind him. Follow the guides' instructions," they repeated as they walked.

Soon the flagman came into view, and those few people needing to go west gathered behind him with the chaotic efficiency one would expect from a crowd having generally the same interests. Some faced east, waiting for the flagman to be sure he had all his travelers. Some faced west. Some moved way west, hoping to be in the front of the group. Animals and people milled about waiting to move on.

Finally, the flagman put his flag away, and the few men in charge of this part of the group called for all to rise and be ready to move. The people and the animals headed west and waited for those in front of them to move on. So they did.

"Well, Mary, this is the last part of our journey," said her Uncle. "Won't it be good to have it over," he said without a question in his voice.

"I am so anxious to see Elizabeth. I have seen her before, I guess, but I cannot remember that. It was very long ago."

"Yes, she came to Nazareth one time about thirteen years ago or so. You were just about walking at that time. You will like her. She is a very good woman," said Jonathan, remembering younger years with his nieces, the sibling fights, and the loving moments that make up family life.

After a few hours, they came to a road marker, a group of similar stones stacked in a tidy pyramid. "Here is the marker where we have to leave the group and move up this road," Jonathan said.

They bid goodbye to the people they had walked with, waved to Samuel's guides and headed off for Elizabeth's house. Up a hill, down a hill and up again they trudged.

"I think we will see their house over this next hill," said Jonathan. As they crested the hill, Jonathan said "There it is."

He pointed to a house on the left side of the road a few hundred paces up. Mary stopped to look—and to rest a moment—and looked at her Uncle with a silent smile of excitement. Then they began the last steps of their journey.

THE GREETING

It was a typical mud brick house with a little more wood than most city houses. It had a wooden door, which city houses generally did not. But out here, wild animals were a more pressing concern, and a door was very important. Mary saw the garden in the back and the other signs of life. As they approached, they called out: "Hello, Zachary! Hello, Elizabeth!"

Elizabeth was inside working with the food for the evening meal. She wondered who it could be at her door. Inside her, her baby moved very forcefully. "Oh, baby!" she said to him, "We have visitors!" In her heart and mind a flash of intuition burst on her consciousness. This baby is responding to the voice we have heard. It is the voice of a woman who is with child as well. It is the woman who will bear the son of the Most High to ransom Israel.

She went to her door and opened it. She stared with disbelief at her brother. "Jonathan!" she yelled. "What are you doing here!?"

"I can go back if you like," said the jokester.

"Oh, Jonathan, of course not," she said. "Oh, please come in. Have you come all the way from Nazareth?"

"Yes, we did. And this is Hannah's Mary. We heard of your being with child, and Mary has come to help you in your time of need."

"Mary!" Elizabeth said. "The last time I saw you, you were just starting to walk! And now look at you. What a lovely woman you have become."

"Oh, Elizabeth, thank you," Mary said, feeling a bit self-conscious. "I'm just me. I'm only Mary."

"And you say you are here to help me with my baby?"

"Yes! Mother and I thought it would be good for you and for me," said Mary.

Elizabeth looked at the young woman and her mature youthful charm. "What a dear thing to offer, Mary; you especially. Of all women, you are the most blessed and blessed is the fruit of your womb. How is it that the mother of my Lord should come to me? As soon as I heard your voice, the child in me leapt for joy. Yes, blessed is she who believed that the promise made her by the Lord would be fulfilled."

Jonathan tried to process what he was hearing. Mary? With child? As he tried to make sense of this, Mary said,

> My soul proclaims the greatness of the Lord
> and my spirit rejoices in God my savior;
> because He has looked upon His lowly handmaid.
> Yes, from this day forward, all generations
>   shall call me blessed,
> for the Almighty has done great things for me.
> Holy is His name,

and His mercy reaches from age to age for those who fear
     Him.
He has shown the power of His arm,
 He has routed the proud of heart.
He has pulled down princes from their thrones and
     exalted the lowly.
The hungry He has filled with good things, the rich He has
     sent empty away.
He has come to the help of Israel, His servant,
     mindful of his mercy
—according to the promise He made to our ancestors—
of His mercy to Abraham and his descendants forever.

In the ensuing silence, Jonathan stared at Elizabeth, and then at Mary. Eventually, he said, "I hope you will explain all this to me. Mary, are you with child too?"

Mary looked sheepishly at him and said, "Yes, I am. I was visited by an angel some weeks ago now. He told me that I was to bear a son and that he would be great, and all sorts of things. And he told me that Elizabeth, in her older age, was also with child. I knew that before we visited you at your house."

Jonathan looked on in silence. Finally, he simply said, "Wow!" He realized that he would learn more about this, but only in due time would the information play out. "Do you need to rest, Mary?" he asked.

"I could use a little rest, but I feel alright overall," she said.

Jonathan looked at her in a whole new light. Her face, her person, her presence were all changed in his mind in a way that he could not yet explain. As with her mother, her father, her in-laws, and her husband, this story of hers, in this brief insight he had into it, struck him silent. He had to think it through.

Elizabeth said, "Come and rest on the mat. Take a nap if you wish. Refresh yourself. We will have plenty of time to talk later. I am sure Zachary will make a new place for you later as well, but for now you just rest. I will prepare a small meal, since midday is approaching, and have it ready for you when you are rested."

"Oh, Elizabeth," said Mary, "I am supposed to be here to help you, and now we are just making more work for you."

"No, no, no," said Elizabeth. "I am fine right now, and you are worn out from your great journey. You rest. Besides," she said, smiling at her brother, "we have this big man here and we can make him do all the work."

Jonathan, in a long drawl, said, "Oh, you think so!" smiling as well.

"Come, Jonathan," Elizabeth said, guiding him to another area of the house. "You can rest over here."

"A good plan," said the brother.

Elizabeth prepared the meal of refreshing cucumber and goat cheese, some flatbread, olives, and watered wine. She bustled about the house adapting it for her visitors. In her mind and heart, she also adapted. What a blessing, she thought, to have her brother here and her dear cousin. There would be so much to catch up on. She wanted to go in and wake them up, but knew, of course, that she would have to wait for them to rest.

As the midday began to age, Mary came into the kitchen area with her arms folded and looking sleepy and blinky.

"Oh, you dear girl," said Elizabeth with a smile. Mary's childhood was still a small part of her, and she accepted a familial older-cousin hug. "Come, I have food for you." They moved to a low table and Mary sat on the floor. "I'll go kick that brother of mine and get him up," she said. They had a long-standing brother-sister relationship of jesting love for each other. She indulged in, and Jonathan allowed her, this game of comic violation of the role of woman in society.

Elizabeth went to Jonathan and said, "Come on, brother. Rest is over." Jonathan took a deep breath, gathered his strength and resolve and then quickly sat up. He contemplated crashing back down but stood up and said to his sister, "That was a good rest. I dreamt and dreamt about camels and caravans."

"Well, for now," said Elizabeth, "we have cucumbers and cumquats, and other things for you. Come and eat."

As they entered the next room, Mary said, "These cucumbers are like a rain shower in my mouth."

Jonathan sat down, and Elizabeth joined them. They caught up with their hunger and the opportunity to talk grew.

"So," said Jonathan, ruefully. "You ladies have some explaining to do. What is going on here?"

They began to share their stories.

Elizabeth said, "I have long realized that I was barren, and so has the community. Zachary and I have prayed so much for a child, but we have not conceived. Now we are both advanced in years. The community always looked down on us, you know, giving us that sympathetic look. Then, on one Sabbath, when Zachary was performing the priestly service in the House of Prayer, it was his lot to offer incense. He went into the Temple of the Lord. As the congregation was praying without, at the time for incense, an angel appeared to him. He said it was on the right side of the altar of incense. Zachary saw him and fear fell upon him. But the angel said to him,

Fear not, Zachary, for your prayer is heard. Your wife Elizabeth shall bear you a son, and you shall call his name John. He will bring you a lot of joy, and many will rejoice at his birth. He will be great before the Lord. He will drink no wine nor strong drink. He will be filled with the Holy Ghost, even from his mother's womb. He will convert many of the children of Israel to the Lord, their God. He will go before him in the spirit and power of Elias and will turn the hearts of the fathers to the children, and the incredulous to the wisdom of the just, to prepare for the Lord a perfect people.

"Well, Zachary stared at the angel. He kept staring, and the angel saw that he was slow to believe this startling prediction. As a result, the angel told him that, as punishment for his doubt, he would be struck dumb until the promise was fulfilled. And so it was. He was just beginning his week of duty in the temple. After his duty was done, he came home. He has not been able to speak since."

Mary then told her story once again. What a blessing to be telling it with joy and to a loving audience. As the stories came together, Jonathan realized that this was a momentous story—if it were true.

"Well," he said, "we have a number of years before these children will take their places among the people. We will have to walk in God's own time. First," he said, in his jesting way, "we have to see if they are boys when they are born—"

The ladies looked at him with false anger, enjoying his humor. Weeks passed, and Jonathan helped Zachary with various tasks around the house and the property. Mary and Jonathan came to be recognized in the town. Elizabeth grew great with her child, and her time, day by day, drew nearer. More and more, she allowed Mary to help her with going to the village market for the daily foodstuffs and water and with preparing the meals and with various other tasks around the house. Elizabeth, of course, helped as much as she could.

"You need to rest more," said Mary one day. "Your baby is very near."

"Oh, I'll be all right," said Elizabeth. Generally, she was. She had good energy and was very much involved in the work of the house. However, more and more, she asked Mary to do things that were strenuous or awkward. Likewise, Mary was sure that her increasing service was truly helping Elizabeth in these the last few weeks of her pregnancy.

One day, Elizabeth spoke up and said, "I think we are close now. It has been close to nine months and I know I am ready, even if this baby is not. If he does not come soon, I will have to live outside because the house will not be big enough for me to get in," she said, and she and Mary shared a good laugh at that. "I have arranged with a midwife to assist me in the birth," she told Mary. "We will go and meet her this afternoon. She has explained many things to me, some I did not want to hear. Many women have great difficulties in delivering a child and often do not survive the process.

It is rare, but it can happen. It is always in your mind, she says, until the child is finally born. However, one of the normal things is for the water to break and seep out. So, she told me to wear a loincloth for when it happens. I've started to do that today."

"The angel told me that, with God, all things are possible," said Mary. "We must do all we can, and trust Him after that."

"Yes, that's true. In their own ways, these babies are special, and we must trust the Lord to care for them and for us. It's still scary," said Elizabeth.

"I'll be here with you," said Mary.

"And that will be very good," said Elizabeth, "Very, very good."

They embraced side-to-side and put their faces together, sharing the genuine fondness for each other that had grown during these weeks.

"Come outside with me." said Elizabeth. "I will show you where the midwife lives. Her name is Naomi. You will like her. She is one of the most caring people I know."

There was no trained physician in this small town of Ain-Karim, five miles southwest of Jerusalem. The people relied on the noted midwife, Naomi, wife of Jacob, who lived on the western edge of the town. She had been active in her profession for a number of years. She was literate and read such birthing writings as she could get. She was regarded as an intelligent woman devoted to her work and, as a result, was valued and respected by almost everyone. It was ironic that she herself had no child, but her many years of work brought with them a well deserved reputation. Many of her patients said that she brought them comfort and confidence with a tender but no-nonsense approach. She did not tend to use the superstitious practices of many other midwives.

Mary and Elizabeth went to the front of the house, and Elizabeth pointed up the hill to the houses that gathered at the edge of town, just a few hundred yards away.

"Do you see the second house up there on the right? That is the house of Jacob and Naomi. When we need her, someone will have to go to her and tell her. I assume Jonathan will run to her and bring her, but we all have to be ready."

Later that day, as they were preparing the evening meal, Elizabeth felt her water seeping into the cloth and said with a start, "Op! Mary! It's happened!"

With them both being novices at this, they each got a bit excited. Mary went to Elizabeth's side and took her arm. "What do we do now?" asked Mary.

"Zachary! Jonathan!" called Mary. They did not immediately appear, and she cried out again. Jonathan came running it, and Zachary soon followed. Jonathan went to his sister's other side. Elizabeth said, "Someone go for the midwife." she said. "Jonathan, you go."

Zachary moved in to take Jonathan's place, and Jonathan headed off to the midwife's house. He ran all the way, taking a stride that he felt would get him there but not collapse him. He approached and called out, "Jacob! Naomi! Hello!" He got to their door, and they were coming to it in response to his calls. Having met him before at Elizabeth's house, they knew him.

"Jonathan! Hello. Is it Elizabeth?" Naomi asked.

"Yes. She says to come now."

"What has happened so far?" she asked.

"I don't really know," he said. "They just told me to come for you."

"Is she in any trouble?" Naomi said as she gathered her kit. "Tell me what you saw."

"She and Mary called out to me and Zachary. We both came running in and Mary was helping her, holding her right arm and—"

"So, she was standing?" asked Naomi.

"Yes, yes." said Jonathan breathlessly, interpreting Naomi's words as a good sign.

"Very well," said Naomi. "It's probably just her water. I'll go and see how things are going. I'll probably be back soon, Jacob," she said to her husband.

They left Jacob's house and made their way to Zachary's. When they arrived, Elizabeth was sitting on a chair and Mary and Zachary were standing by.

Elizabeth and Naomi greeted each other, and Naomi settled into her leadership role. "How's it going?" she asked, using the professional's open-ended question.

"I think it's just my water," said Elizabeth. "There's not much else going on."

"Any contractions, even little ones?" asked Naomi.

"I don't think so, but I'm not sure. You know, there are lots of times when there are little contractions, but they just go away."

"Well, yes. Also, many times the water breaks but the baby does not come for many hours or even some days. I'll stay with you for a while and see if there are any signs that things are moving along. We may have a little more waiting to do," said Naomi.

"I know I am ready," said Elizabeth, smiling.

"Well, you let me know if there is any contraction that you feel." said Naomi. They all settled down into small talk and waited. "No matter how many times throughout history this pageant has played out, it is still a very intense time, isn't it?" observed Naomi.

Time wore on, and Mary asked, "How are you feeling, Elizabeth?"

"I feel fine. There is nothing going on," she said, looking to Naomi. Naomi remarked: "As I said, it can sometimes be days after the water breaks before the baby starts to come. I think that, since everything seems still to be calm, I will go back home and wait to hear from you. Alright?"

All agreed, Naomi left for her home. Mary spoke up. "Shall I prepare the evening meal? It is time for it and we need our strength," she said, sounding in her own mind a lot like her mother.

"I will eat lightly in case this boy changes his mind," said Elizabeth.

The four of them ate their meal and, with the setting sun, settled down for the evening. Sleep came to them. In her advanced pregnancy, Elizabeth slept well enough, but woke often and changed position to get some comfort. In the very early morning, she woke to the sense of pressure around the baby. She was instantly alert and evaluating her experiences. She did not want to react too soon, so she waited. Soon the compression relaxed and so did she. As she was drifting back to sleep, the compression built again. Ah, yes, you boy. You are coming, aren't you? she said to herself.

She poked Zachary and told him, "I think this baby's coming now." Zachary sat up with a start, indicating with his makeshift sign language, "Now!? Really?"

"Yes, yes!" said Elizabeth.

That, of course, rang through the silent house and woke Mary and Jonathan. Soon everyone was awake and hovering over Elizabeth.

THE BABY

"Shall I go for Naomi?" asked Jonathan.

"I think so," said Elizabeth. "The squeezing is building, stronger each time. It's time, I believe."

Jonathan left for Naomi's house. Again, he jogged to the home near the edge of town and called for her as he approached it. Since it was so early, he waited outside for someone to come out. Soon Jacob, her husband, came out and said that she would soon be ready. In a few moments she appeared with her equipment and said, "Okay, Jonathan?"

Jonathan nodded and turned to go with Naomi. "I will be home when I can," she said to Jacob. In her mind she had concerns very different from her professional tone. She had seen many births, some relatively simple, and some very, very difficult. Elizabeth's age and lack of prior pregnancies were causes for concern.

Naomi's supplies included clean, fresh olive oil; various ointments to be warmed and applied to the body; soft sea sponges; pieces of wool; swaddling bandages for the infant; a pillow on which to which to place the infant; things to smell, such as pennyroyal, apples, quinces, and lemon, in case the mother fainted; and her midwife's stool.

"In my discussions with Elizabeth, I told her that we would need two beds, a hard one for use during labor and a soft one for rest after delivery, or else we could use a delivery chair. I think she told me that Zachary had gotten a chair for the delivery. Do you know if they are available?" Naomi asked Jonathan.

"They have the chair and a bed for resting after the baby comes," said Jonathan.

"Good. That should be fine." said Naomi. "I can't imagine making her sit on Zachary's lap for the delivery."

Jonathan laughed in agreement, catching her edgy joking. He was thankful that it was not a problem they would face. Naomi's experience indicated that normal delivery was easier when the mother sat upright.

When they arrived at the house, the three were standing, Elizabeth supported by Mary and Zachary. Elizabeth was apparently dealing with another contraction.

"Oh, Naomi, thank you for coming. I know it will be soon," she said through a tense throat.

Naomi spoke up. "I am here now, and we'll just take this one step at a time. Now, where is the chair?"

Jonathan looked at Zachary, and Zachary looked at Jonathan.

"Do you know where it is?" asked Jonathan.

"Oh, yes," said Zachary. He went and got the chair and set it behind Elizabeth.

"I need you to sit down so I can check to see how big the opening is. With that I can tell about how far along we are," said Naomi.

The two men helped Elizabeth to sit and then left the room.

"I need some water warmed up," she told them as they left, "and this oil. Please make the water hot, but the oil just warm enough to be comfortable. Bring the oil to me as soon as it is ready. I will need the water right when the baby is born."

The men went to the oven to refresh the fire and warm up the water and the oil.

Naomi applied olive oil to her left index finger and moved Elizabeth's clothing up. She examined the cervix and found the opening to be still only slightly larger than her finger. "We will wait until it's about the size of an egg before we get serious about this," she said. "Mary, you sit behind her and let her rest against you."

Naomi helped Elizabeth to a sitting position, and Mary took her station behind her. Naomi began to ease the labor tightness with gentle massage of Elizabeth's abdomen. "As we go on," she said, "we will use a cloth soaked in warm olive oil and lay it on you here and down over the opening. I will work the opening some with my finger, but mostly it will be at its own time. When it is big enough, we will move to the chair and get to work."

"And what is this now?" asked Elizabeth, starting to show the effects of the work she had already done. "I meant that as a bit of a joke," she said, "I didn't mean to snap at you, Naomi."

"Don't you worry. This is all new to you, and you will find yourself doing all kinds of new things, including snapping at me. The only rule I have is that you can't hit," Naomi said, smiling. "I know that this is work, too, and you are doing fine," Naomi went on. "But, as you know, there's more to come."

There was a moment of time when a contraction had receded, and they were waiting for the next one. Naomi took the time to explain further. "Now, for the actual delivery, I will need Mary to hold Elizabeth around from the back. You will kneel behind the chair. You need to make sure that she does not overpower you, and you need to make sure she does not fall to either side. And you," she said, pointing to Elizabeth, "you need to pay attention to that also. You can't fall over either way. Alright?"

Elizabeth nodded, and they began their short wait for the next contraction. Naomi revaluated the inner opening once again and said, "I think after this next contraction, we will try to push."

The contraction came, and Elizabeth stressed with it. "It feels like I am tearing open," she said.

Naomi said, "Everything is fine. You will be amazed at what you can do. Now I want you, Mary, to help Elizabeth to remember to breathe well and not hold her breath except when we push to deliver the baby. Alright? Women often start holding their breath and get dizzy during all the other things going on, and you have to help her remember." Mary nodded her understanding." Also, as you are holding her from behind, I want you to gently help her push the baby down and out. Not too hard, now. We are only helping Elizabeth do what she needs to do."

Naomi saw that Elizabeth's last contraction was over and examined the opening once again. "I can feel his little head and the opening is progressing."

For Mary, it was a strangely intimate thing to hold her cousin's body in her arms, to feel her warmth and her muscular actions, and to smell the odors of her hair and body. Elizabeth's next contraction came, and Naomi told her to push to try to deliver the baby. Naomi worked on the opening slightly to help the baby's head move further, Elizabeth pushed, and Mary gently assisted.

"In these first few contractions I want you to get a feel for the pushing because soon we are going to try to make it happen," said Naomi

"First few?!" protested Elizabeth. "How long will this go on?" Elizabeth was at the edge of her acceptance of this process.

"It's alright. You are doing fine. I've seen many women go through this, and you're doing fine," said the professional. "It is important to rest and regain your body's balance for the next contraction. Alright? Breathe deep and slow until we get ready to push. Tell me when the contraction begins."

"I think it's coming now," said Elizabeth.

At the same time, Jonathan said from just outside the room, "Naomi, the oil is ready."

"Wait, Jonathan," she said. To Elizabeth, she said, "Good. Now, when it builds, we'll push and try to bring the baby out. I don't think he'll come this time but we will try. Alright?" As Elizabeth was nodding, Naomi said to Mary, "You ready, Mary? You know what to do?"

Mary nodded and adjusted her hands over the top of Elizabeth's belly. She could feel the contraction build and waited for Naomi's instructions. Naomi put her hands on Elizabeth also and as the contraction built she said, "Alright, Elizabeth. Make this baby come!"

Elizabeth pushed with all her might. Her face turned a wondrous shade of blue-crimson, and the veins in her forehead stood out like tree branches. Her belly muscles felt like they were on fire, and her tissues like they were tearing open.

Naomi encouraged her, saying "Good! Good! Keep it up a little more, little more." Mary pushed some and the three were a coordinated team. The contraction began to fade, and Elizabeth relaxed with a whoosh of air. "Alright, now," said Naomi. "We made great progress. You're doing fine. Breathe deep and slow and recover yourself. Maybe next time we can do it."

Elizabeth was too exhausted to do anything but obey. Sweat rolled from her face, and her clothing was soaked. Mary whispered to her, "You are doing great. It won't be long. Breathe slow and deep."

Naomi pulled Elizabeth's clothing back down and said, "Alright, Jonathan, please bring the oil in."

Jonathan brought it in a warm clay pot that had been sitting on the oven, and the oil was nicely warmed.

"Thank you, Jonathan," she said, "It looks like I will need the water very soon as well. Please get it and wait outside of the room until I call you in with it, alright?"

"Alright" said Jonathan and he left.

Naomi again lifted Elizabeth's clothing and checked the cervix. It was fully open. The baby's head was visible. "Things are proceeding nicely," she said. "Let me know when the next contraction builds. Now, listen. When the baby comes, I will tell you to stop pushing. No matter what, when I say stop, you must stop. Do you understand?"

Elizabeth nodded, her eyes closed and waiting. In a few moments, Elizabeth said, "It's here."

Naomi put her hands on Elizabeth again and in a few seconds said, "All right. Are we all ready? Come on, Elizabeth, make that baby come!"

Again, Elizabeth pushed. Mary pushed, too, harder this time, feeling more and more confident about her tasks.

Jonathan and Zachary came to the edge of the entrance to the room. They were discreetly out of view, but they could hear everything.

"He's coming. He's coming," said Naomi. The baby's head began to emerge and Naomi said, "Keep going, but soon we will have to stop. Keep going, now. He's coming more." Naomi had her hands wrapped in linen and grasped the baby's head lightly. "A little more," she said, ignoring Elizabeth's crimson face. The baby's head cleared the opening, and she saw the shoulders begin to appear and the baby begin to speed up. "Stop! Stop!" she said.

Elizabeth whooshed a breath and tried to undo everything she had been trying so hard to do up to then. At the same time, the baby's head remained in the linen in Naomi's left hand, and the baby's back and bottom were in her right hand.

"He's out. Good for you, Elizabeth."

Elizabeth's mind registered the relief of her body, that the baby was free, that she was finished with the delivery, and that she was not going to die in this childbirth. Instantly, she cried, "Oh, my baby. How is he?" Everything in her wanted to hold this baby now. She tried to reach out for him and Naomi said, "Hold her, Mary! Not yet, Elizabeth. You must wait just a moment."

Mary tightened her arms around Elizabeth. The older woman relaxed her body, but still she kept asking about her baby, almost frantically, as Naomi examined him.

After a moment that seemed like forever, Naomi said, "He looks fine. I will tie off the cord and cut it, and clean him off, and you can have him. In the meantime, you have to deliver the afterbirth. You and Mary work on that. It will come similarly to the baby, pretty much on its own."

Jonathan deemed that the time had arrived when Naomi would need the water and said, "Naomi, we have the water."

"Wait a moment," said Naomi. Then she said "Mary," and nodded towards Elizabeth's clothing. Mary moved the clothing back down, and Naomi said. "Bring the water, Jonathan."

Naomi set the baby on the cushion and let him rest a bit. Both men gathered at the doorway to the room, like strangers almost, and were amazed and thrilled at what they saw. Naomi cleared the mucus from the baby's nose and mouth, and ensured that he was breathing well. He had let out a series of clarion calls but now was settling down. The men were smiling and staring at this wonder. Naomi spoke up, saying, "We need just a little more privacy right now." The men took their cue and left as Naomi was saying, "It won't be long before you can come back."

She then tied the cord with a woolen string and cut it with a knife from her kit. She tried to gently press the bent cord into the navel. She then cleaned the waxy coating from baby with a moderate amount of fine and powdery salt, mixed with honey and olive oil. She washed it away with warm water and repeated the process a second time.

As she washed him, she checked his ears and the rest of his little self. She made sure to clear the anus of any membranes that might impede regular bowel movements. She also put a little olive oil into his eyes to clear away any birth residue. Finally, she put a small piece of wool soaked with olive oil over the cord.

Naomi was relieved that none of the often-intractable problems she had experienced was going to happen today. There were many remedies that she had heard of also, but she never did anything that she felt was not truly effective and which she felt others might only use to impress their patients. She had heard of providing a drink of mouse dung diluted with rain water and ass's milk for swelling of the breasts. Also, she had heard of rubbing the breasts with sow's blood and goose grease mixed with rose oil and a spider's web, or the fat of bustards, in order to relieve swelling. A poultice of partridge egg ash, zinc oxide ointment, and wax was supposed to keep the breasts firm.

For breasts that inflame to the point of infection and discharge of pus, laying earthworms across the breasts was to draw out the pus, and earthworms drunk with honey wine were supposed to stimulate the flow of milk. Fortunately, this delivery was free of serious trouble so far and extreme measures did not seem to be needed, in Naomi's view of things.

As Naomi had worked, Elizabeth finally delivered the after-birth. Mary and Naomi attended to the cleanup of the patient. Naomi had been careful to keep the water supply clean. With her fourth and fifth piece of cloth, she gave Elizabeth a washing. Finally, she cleaned her sweaty face and hair and put sweet smelling oil on her. Mary secured a change of clothing for her and the readied her for her short journey to the resting bed. Her body dried and the new clothing and loin cloth in place, they assisted her to her feet gently and guided her to the bed. They assisted her down and helped her arrange herself comfortably.

"I want my baby," she said.

"That's good, because now you can have him. More importantly, he can have you. How are you feeling?"

"I am feeling like I just had a baby!" she said in false anger. "And that I have had the help of a dear friend and a great midwife. Thank you so much, you dear people."

Naomi had the baby wrapped in his swaddling linens. He was warm and cozy. His hands were within the linens. His eyes were closed, and he was the picture of peace. She brought the baby to his mother, and she held him for the first time.

"He's so light," she said with surprise. "Are you sure he's all right?"

"I'm sure," said Naomi with a smile for the two of them. "You can nurse him whenever you want to, although he's sleeping now. Let's not disturb him yet. Can the men come back?"

"Oh, sure. Let them come in," said Elizabeth.

Naomi called them and they came in to the room quietly and carefully. Despite their joy, there were careful not to become ritually unclean by contact with any of the birth fluids.

It was a new experience for Zachary. Jonathan had been there before with the births of his boys. Everyone settled in, Zachary by his wife and new son and the rest where they could find room. The moments flowed like a gentle stream of quiet around occasional tender comments.

The day wore on, and Naomi felt that she could leave the new family on its own.

Mary spoke up and said, "You haven't eaten in a long time. Midday has come and gone. Can I get you something to eat?"

Naomi politely explained that she had plenty at home and that she would be fine. Mary insisted that it would be no trouble and the etiquette resulted in Naomi staying for a light meal of vegetables and fruits and a little watered wine. Mary prepared it for all, and they all savored both the meal and the moment. Naomi then left for home, and the family began integrating the new little man into the routine duties that still had to be done.

THE RITUALS

Over the ensuing week, Jonathan assisted Mary and Zachary with the work of the house. At the same time, the household was preparing to take the baby to his presentation and Elizabeth to her purification. This was the time of her confinement, and all who associated with her in this time would need ritual purification after the time was over.

On the eighth day they went to the Temple to circumcise the child, and the leaders of the ceremony began to call him by his father's name, Zachary.

Elizabeth answered, "No, no. His name is John."

They then said to her, "There is no one of your kin that is called John." They made sign to his father, asking what the boy's name would be.

Zachary asked for a writing tablet and he wrote, saying: "John is his name."

They all hububbed about this. At the same moment, Zachary, his penalty served and his faithfulness rewarded, said:

Blessed be the Lord the God of Israel,
He has come to his people and set them free.

He has raised up for us a mighty savior
born of the house of his servant David.
Through his holy prophets he promised of old that he would save us from
our enemies, from the hands of all who hate us.
He promised to show mercy to our fathers and to remember his holy covenant.
This was the oath he swore to our father Abraham: to set us free from the
hands of our enemies, free to worship him without fear, holy and righteous
in his sight
all the days of our life.

You my child, shall be called the prophet of the Most High;
for you will go before the Lord to prepare his way,
to give his people knowledge of salvation
by the forgiveness of their sins.
In the tender compassion of our God
the dawn from on high shall break upon us,
to shine on those who dwell in darkness and the shadow of death,
and to guide our feet into the way of peace.

The little group stood in rapt silence, thinking, looking at Zachary, the baby, the temple, and wondering at this most unusual thing—that Zachary had been unable to speak these past many months and now was saying these amazing words. Soon, the baby cried out again, and all eyes turned to him. The power of the moment turned to smiles that came from and they returned to the God they loved. They handed the baby over to the priests, and they performed the ancient ritual.

After the ceremony, more mundane concerns returned to the group, and they began to review their plans for the rest of the day. They went out to the streets and followed Zachary. He was, after all, the most experienced of all of them about this city. He led them to a street a few blocks away from the Temple where there was a tidy whitewashed building among the others. He had arranged some time ago to have a place for his group to rest a while, before visiting a few local shops and returning home with Elizabeth—and now baby John. Tomorrow they would celebrate with their friends and neighbors in their village. They arrived and made their introductions, especially of the newly born and blessed boy. Jacob fussed appropriately over him and blessed him and his father and mother.

The shop was filled with the aroma of baked delicacies. Jacob proudly showed his handiwork, breads of various kinds, pastries made with fruit honeys as well as bee honey, and nuts and fruits.

"It is easy to see why people love to come here," said Zachary, still quietly marveling at his returned voice. "We are going to rest a short while and then go out to shop for things for our feast at home tomorrow. Surely we will take some of these beautiful things. Where do you recommend, we go for some mutton or, maybe, some beef, if we can afford it?"

"Oh, I know a wonderful place," he said, looking at the visitors. "It is only a few streets from here. It is the place of Aaron and Tobias, who prepare the most wonderful lamb." Motioning with his hands, he indicated the way. "You go two lanes up this way and five more to the left. You will not have to ask for them; the aromas will lead you right to them," he said with a deep laugh. "They usually are roasting something to attract people to their shop."

"Let us go up to see the rooms for now," Zachary said.

"Certainly," said Jacob, and he led them to a sturdy ladder that led them up to the second floor of the building. There were two plastered and painted rooms. It would be quite nice for this afternoon in Jerusalem. The rooms were modestly but quaintly appointed. Jacob had put four chairs in the one room, for the group to sit and talk together. They all sat with sighs of relaxation, and marveled at this day, the welcoming of this new person into their community.

Then they noticed pastries on a small table and water in a pitcher and bowls to drink from. "Oh, look what Jacob has done for us," said Zachary.

They enjoyed the pastries and refreshed themselves with the water. Jonathan looked at Mary and said, "Well, it won't be long now until you have your own child. One boy, so far," he said, smiling knowingly at her.

Mary, reading her uncle's humor, winked at him, surprising herself with her new air of confidence and maturity.

Elizabeth put her own fidgeting infant to her breast, under her clothing.

"I know," Mary said. "It will be wonderful for these boys to grow up knowing each other. What fun it will be to share their growing."

After some minutes, baby John was quiet, and Elizabeth put him up to her shoulder. His little mouth popped a quiet burp, which did not disturb his sleep. Mary took him and put him very carefully on the soft matting Jacob's wife had arranged in the other room. Everyone would listen and respond to the slightest noise he might make, but for now, they savored the luxury of this afternoon of rest.

Mary came back and sat again. She took a deep relaxing breath and said, "How wonderful are your works, oh Lord."

"Amen, amen," they all said.

Soon, without planning it, they were all napping in their chairs.

After a while, baby John squawked a bit, and everyone awoke. Mary and Elizabeth both rose to attend to him.

"I'll get him," said Elizabeth. "You're the expectant mother now. It's your turn to start letting others help you," she said to Mary with a smile.

"Oh, I'm all right," said Mary as they left the room together. "It's still quite a while. I'm hardly showing," she said quietly to her cousin.

They returned with the boy and sat with the two men. They talked leisurely and prepared for their walk to see what Aaron and Tobias and the other shops had to offer.

Jacob was right. The aromas of roasting lamb filled the streets as they walked past the fourth lane on the way that Jacob told them to go. They looked ahead to the fifth lane and a bit past the corner saw a wooden lamb-shaped sign on the front of a building. They walked on. They crossed the fifth lane and passed a couple of buildings. Soon they could read the sign. It simply said "Aaron and Tobias." It seemed to imply, "If you don't know why you're here, we can't help you." The visitors all knew why they were there.

The group went in and they were greeted by the two proprietors. Zachary spoke for his group and explained that Jacob had recommended them.

"Well, then," said Aaron. "We shall not disappoint you, or our friend Jacob." He gave a broad smile and extended his hand in greeting.

"We are planning a feast for tomorrow in honor of our young John's circumcision," Zachary said, proudly motioning toward the baby.

"Well, is beef in order?" asked Aaron.

"Oh, it would be if we could afford it," answered Zachary, "but we will be serving as many as twenty people. I think we need to stay with mutton."

"I'll tell you what," said Aaron. "I will provide you with a good twenty-serving lamb roast and a ten-serving beef roast and you can give your guests a taste of each. You pay only for the lamb. I will make a gift in honor of this new man-child."

"Oh, you need not do that," said Zachary. "We will pay for all of it."

"Ah, what will Jacob say? He will say I treated his friends like Romans!" Aaron said with a definite growl in his voice, and a smile on his face. His position was clear in their regard.

"Your offer is most generous, and we thank you," said Zachary. "It seems there may be some other things we might need for tomorrow," he said with a wink.

Elizabeth and Mary looked over the spices and cheeses that were also available there.

"We have to make sure we can carry it home," said Elizabeth. "I guess we can carry the spices, right, Zachary?" quipped Jonathan. They reviewed the items for sale and bought judiciously only things that they could not get in their own village. They also bought items for a lunch that they needed before they began their trek: slices of salted dried lamb and wedges of cheese and enough watered wine for the group. Their purchases made, they each took a share of the load and wondered among themselves about where to find a place to eat their late lunch. Tobias told them, "We have a small plaza a few lanes up on the way to Ephraim. There is a well and there are trees for shade. I will show you they way." They all were ready. They thanked Aaron and told him, "Jacob will not be disappointed. We have been most well served by his advice to come here." Aaron said "Thank you, Zachary. I hope to see you again soon."

They left the shop with their meats, spices, and cheeses. Tobias walked them a few lanes to the west and the plaza appeared. It was a perfect place for their lunch. Tobias bid them Godspeed and left to go back to the shop. "What a good bit of advice Jacob gave us," Zachary said. "Yes, yes," said Jonathan. They parsed out their lunches and shared the watered wine. Elizabeth nursed John. Each of the party made sure they drank some water and had their water flask filled. They visited the outhouse available in the plaza and set out on the road to Ephraim for their hour-long walk to their village. Once home, they would eat a light evening meal and retire early. There was a big day tomorrow.

HOME

When they arrived at Zachary's home, Mary prepared a small sustaining meal. They ate, cleaned up, tended to John, and readied some things for the work of tomorrow's celebration. Then they retired for the evening.

Morning came before sunrise for baby John and his mother; a couple of times, in fact. She and Mary attended to his little noises and enjoyed the quietness and the slow brightening of the morning. Each of them, in turn, went out to the outhouse for their morning eliminations or washed their faces. Baby John was fed and cleaned. The men picked up on the morning activity and rose with the sun. They performed their morning toils as well.

Soon, after a functional breakfast of flatbread, fruit, and water, all were all busy in preparation for the day's festivities. Mary and Elizabeth bundled up baby John, and headed off to the well to get the day's water. Zachary and Jonathan started the oven fire.

Today they would gladly incur the expense of charcoal for its more uniform, intense, smoke-free heat. Mary prepared the clay cooking pans for the lamb and the beef, and spread the spices on them. On the lamb went a paste of fenugreek, mint, and anise, which she had ground in a mortar along with liberal doses of pepper. The cooking pan would have a good amount of water in it to return moisture to the dried meat and reduce its saltiness during the covered portion of the cooking time. Cooked with the meats in the oven would be the vegetables: lots of cabbage, turnips, and onions were cut into bite-sized pieces and roasted in the covered meat pans with the meat and water.

Zachary had secured wines made from grapes as well as some wine made from figs and spiced with cinnamon and clove. There were also cheeses made from goat milk, primarily, some fresh and soft, soaked in brine, and some well aged, toothsome, and aromatic.

The menu also contained Jacob's breads made from leavened wheat flour and other grains and topped with sesame seed or poppy seed. There was olive oil spiced with salt, pepper, and garlic for dipping the bread.

More substantial grain cakes were made from coarsely ground oat or barley mixed with finer wheat flour, butter and salt, and spiced with cinnamon or anise.

There were cut fruits, such as apples, pears, and apricots mixed with a dressing of date honey, raisin honey, or bee honey and lemon, which kept the fruits from turning brown. Pomegranate was pulled into small sections and placed in a bowl for people to take. They set out bowls of almonds, walnuts, and pistachios.

As noon approached, the aromas of the roasting meats and vegetables filled the air. Preparations were well under way.

Soon there was a call from outside: "Hello Elizabeth! Hello." It was Elizabeth's friend, Beulah, from a few doors away. "I came to see what I could do to help before the guests start arriving."

Elizabeth greeted her by saying, "Oh, what a friend you are. You don't need to do anything. You just sit and be comfortable."

"I've brought some things for the celebration," said Beulah.

"Oh, you dear!" said Elizabeth.

Beulah pulled from her bag a number of things: date pastries she had made, a large bowl with fresh salad greens and vegetables ready to cut and dress, and a couple of small wine jugs. The women's oos and ahs, thank-yous and you're welcomes, laughter, hugs, and smiles filled the kitchen.

"Guests will arrive soon," observed Mary. "What a table we will have!"

They continued putting out the final items. Within the hour, many neighbors and friends arrived with additional food offerings and gifts for baby John. Greetings and chatter filled the house. The afternoon matured. People blended from one conversation group to another, making new acquaintances, renewing old ones, putting the cares of the workaday world aside for a few blessed hours and feeling the promise of the future wrapped up in this new baby.

As evening arrived, like a fire burning low, one person or family left at one point, another later, and little by little the home became more and more quiet. Soon all the guests had bid their blessings and left for their own homes. The meaning of the home of Zachary and Elizabeth was now layered with a new memory; the humanity and life within it was refreshed and the history of this mud-brick structure was deepened and enriched.

The four of them worked at cleaning up and getting themselves to the point where they could rest some. They were exhausted and yet full of a quiet, satisfied joy. Their friends had been blessed and had also been blessings. They would remember this day forever. The next morning, a new normalcy filled the household. Old routines resumed, although every moment was seasoned by the awareness of the new baby in the house. As they ate a breakfast, Jonathan spoke first about what they all were thinking. "Well, Mary, we have only a few days before we leave for Nazareth. Jacob was very helpful in advising us how to join up with a northbound caravan. We are getting to be quite the travelers. I'll bet you will be glad to get home again, won't you."

Mary said, "I have such a mixture of longing to go home and longing to stay with you and this new baby. But, I know my visit must be over. I have responsibilities of my own that are beginning to press on my mind. I have a new husband and especially now, I have to prepare for my own baby."

She felt in her heart a slow transition from comfort in these surroundings to the eagerness to get the next journey over and to be home again.

"Elizabeth, this visit has been a blessing beyond my dreams," she said. "To be here with you, to help you with this baby, to see the wonders God has wrought in our midst—it's just more than I can say. I have come to love you like a mother, like a sister, like—I don't know. We are very specially related now, and nothing will take that away."

They looked at each other, and small tears dripped from their lashes. Elizabeth said, "When you came here, I thought of you as just a girl. Now I know that you are a woman of great stature. I will always cherish the memory of this visit and hope that we can see each other often as these children grow to manhood. You are a blessing already to anyone you meet. May you stay close to God."

They quietly contemplated this moment for some time. Finally, Jonathan adopted an air of grave importance and said to Mary, "I still say, it will be quite a surprise, if this baby of yours is a girl."

Mary was used to her uncle's joking by now. She tried to stifle her laughter, but it only made it more intense. The group found the laughter infectious. They laughed at the joke, at Mary's efforts to stifle her own laughter, and even at their own laughter. Mary had grown in her unquestioning faith in God's providence for her and for His people. She remembered the depths of her despair, but saw them as in the past. Now, this impossibility was so real to her that laughter was the only proper response.

Finally, they all prepared to retire. Mary lay on her mat and contemplated this visit. She imagined the journey home, and the home that Joseph was preparing for them. She imagined her own term and childbirth. Perhaps Zachary and Elizabeth would be able to come to Nazareth and share in it as she had done here. She reflected on how grand it will be to provide a grandson to her mother and father, and to have them all around at that time. Thought began to mix with dream in her mind. In her last waking moment, her heart overflowed with her favorite phrase, "How wonderful are your works, oh, Lord."

THE END

ACKNOWLEDGEMENTS

ACKNOWLEDGEMENTS

en.wikipedia.org/wiki/Shalosh_regalim

https://en.wikipedia.org/wiki/Stone_Age#Lower_Paleolithic
L.S.B. Leakey, Adam's Ancestors (4th ed. 1960);
M.C. Burkitt, The Old Stone Age (4th ed. 1963);
K.P. Oakley, Man the Tool-Maker (5th ed. 1963);
F. Bordes, The Old Stone Age (tr. 1968).

McKenzie, Dictionary of the Bible, Bruce Publishing, Milwaukee, 1965
www.ccel.org/ccel/easton/ebd2.html?term=synagogue
www.ccel.org/ccel/smith_w/bibledict.html?term=synagogue
www.newadvent.org/cathen/14379b.htm
www.myjewishlearning.com/history/Ancient_and_Medieval_History/539_BCE-632_CE/Palestine_in_the_Hellenistic_Age/Synagogue_and_Study_House.shtml
;
The Life and Times of Jesus the Messiah, Alfred Edersheim, 1883
www.jewishencyclopedia.com/view.jsp?letter=M&artid=523
www.revivaltheology.com/EarlyOberlinCD/CD/edersheim
www.exploitz.com/Israel-Climate-cg.php
www.orthodox.co.uk/concepti.htm
Helios, New Series 13(2), 1986, pp. 69-84)
Midwives and Maternity Care in the Roman World, Valerie French
The Catholic Encyclopedia, Volume VI; Copyright © 1909 by Robert Appleton Company; Online Edition Copyright © 2003

by K. Knight; Nihil Obstat, September 1, 1909. Remy Lafort, Censor; Imprimatur. +John M. Farley, Archbishop of New York

ABOUT THE AUTHOR

Tom Atzberger is a native of Mentor, Ohio, and a forty-plus-year resident of Columbus, Ohio. He is married to Christina (Kwiecien), whom he met at John Carroll University and with whom he has helped raise Joseph, Elizabeth, and John. Tom is an attorney by training and is a retired supervisor of stockbrokers.

Tom spent the years from 1964 to 1967 in the college level of the Catholic seminary of the Cleveland Diocese, named for St. Charles Borromeo. His faith has always been his guiding star. His inspiration for this work came from his life experience as a husband, father, uncle, neighbor, and relative of many in his extended family, a life experience we all share. His sentiment is that it is in our daily living we find our vocations and work out our salvation. It was just the same for Mary.

What God calls us to is His choice. We do not earn any of it. But we do complete His will by our "yes" to the life of virtue to which we are called, by responding to life in that yes, and by our faith in His control of our temporal and eternal destinies.

Tom wrote this book to present a personal, family feeling of our relationship to Mary, and hopes that you get the same comfortable closeness with her from this book. While we all are in awe of what God has done through her, we are also each no less called and no less capable of sainthood. It is instructive to think of Mary not only as our Queen, but as our sister as well.

ENDORSEMENTS

Thank you for writing this book. I never looked at Mary this way.
At times, I was almost in tears.
A friend, Henry Pope of Albuquerque, NM.

It seems well written, and follows in detail to the Bible story, as I
remember, of her young life. You seem to make her come alive
with all of the probable detailed added events during the periods
that the New Testament does not include. It seemed so real
because she is not portrayed as some special divine person but as a
child of her time growing into maturity. She seemed to be a very
sensitive and willing to accept everything that life including God
offered her. I could not but wonder if some if not most of the
teachings were more reflective of the author's thinking, than
actual Jewish teachings.

Basically, I thought it is a very good book, about a very sensitive
subject that was well worth reading to help understand this major
historical person.
Rev. Jim Calvert of Marietta, Ohio

I like it. You did a great job and it is very interesting. It piques my
interest for more.
Cheryl Brown, Financial Adviser